Gaea & the Night Witch

Gaea & the Night Witch

The Night Witch Series
A Widow's Watch Novel
~Book 1~

Mark E. Welch

ISBN: 979-8-9986232-0-2
Library of Congress Control Number: 2023907840

The Grimoire

Beware of the Grimoire, as it serves as a guide for practitioners of dark magic, providing them with the knowledge and tools needed to perform magical rituals and spells that enable evil deeds.

Dark magic shares the same capabilities as regular magic, though it appears slightly more potent. Unlike regular magic, dark magic is not limited by Circle laws, allowing witches bound within circles to use their dark magic independently.

Dark magic users possess immunity to magic negation, meaning their magic cannot be stolen or canceled out. A common application of dark magic is the creation of a dark circle, which permits the user to access the Underworld. However, if used improperly, the disturbed spirits can cause severe harm, potentially destroying the user from the inside out.

~ Unknown Necromancer

Table of Contents

CHAPTER 1
Fall Semester

Winter was coming on heavily, and the residents of the town of Orono, Maine, were indifferent to the change. Some who attended the University of Maine felt the change more than others; however, the school also hosted foreign exchange students and those from other parts of the country. The overnight drop in temperature was drastic and led to the campus being full of bundled-up students who hurried to get from building to building and to their next class the following morning. The icy wind seemed to cut to the bone and was quick to numb the senses. The beginning of November was proving to be harsher than most.

Gaea Pender was used to the frigid weather in the state of Maine as she had grown up with it, albeit further south in the town of Cape Neddick. The attractive twenty-two-year-old was in the final year of her undergraduate studies in psychology. Her parents, Bill and Cathy, were delighted with her choice to attend UMO. Her sister Vicky was attending a culinary school in Paris, France, so they were delighted to have one of their daughters nearby. Gaea also enjoyed the closeness. During school breaks, it was a relatively short drive to go home, and her adopted grandparents, Bob and Dottie Pepper, were only a short distance away in Bar Harbor. Gaea couldn't have been happier, other than missing Vicky.

Her brother Aerin was another consideration in Gaea's choice to attend the University of Maine. He was a gifted psychic medium who had just turned twelve. It had taken years, but Gaea had gotten her gift somewhat under control. Upon learning to master a mental discipline known as the charismatic shield, she was no longer under a constant barrage from the dead. She had managed to teach her brother, who seemed to be coping quite well with the spirits, although both still had experiences that they needed to overcome. The life of a psychic medium was a constant challenge.

"Gaea!" A young man ran up and hugged her.

"Hi, Marc. Off to class?"

"Oui, I mean yes," he replied in a light French-Canadian accent. "And you?"

Marc Broussard was from Quebec and had chosen UMO as part of an exchange program with the Université de Montréal. His interest in meteorology led him to study outside of his native Canada to pursue an undergraduate degree. Gaea found the young man attractive. His wavy blond hair and blue eyes contrasted with her chestnut hair and brown eyes. The attraction had been mutual from the day they met three years ago, and it had only grown stronger as time passed.

"I'm on my way to Abnormal Psychology with Professor Parkinson," she replied while adjusting her scarf around her neck.

"He is not in my curriculum, but I hear he is a very good teacher."

"I think he is an exceptional teacher," she replied. "He is very patient but kind of nerdy."

"What profs on campus aren't?

Snow had just started to fall, lightly dusting the couple's shoulders as they walked.

"This crap is coming down from your country," Gaea said with a giggle. "You know that?"

"I beg to differ. I looked at the weather report, and this is coming off the Atlantic, so you can't blame Canada for this one."

"Gaea!" A man called from a few yards away. He was walking in the opposite direction of the couple and smiled and waved.

"Hi, Professor Pickling!" Gaea said.

"Say hi to your dad and tell him I will call him next week about that collaboration."

"Sure! I'm calling him and my mom tonight."

"Great! Stay warm!"

The Professor scurried off toward the literary arts building.

"You know him?" Marc asked in disbelief. "You never told me."

"What is there to tell? He knows my dad, and they are both authors. It's never been a big deal. I've known him for a few years."

Marc sighed. "I guess not. Famous people tend to rub elbows occasionally. We peons can only watch from afar."

"Hey, you have met my dad," Gaea said.

"I know, but he seems to be just an average Joe. You know, down to earth. The kind of man you can just go and have a beer with at the local watering hole."

"He is. Why do you think Professor Pickling is any different?"

"I don't know."

"Well, I do, and he is remarkably like my dad. To be honest, I am surprised he took a position here at UMO. He seems to be the very private type and prefers his pen and notebook to being around the masses. I remember how my father hated book signings.

"They are both brilliant writers and I think I have read everything both have written. So, it sounded to me like they might do a collaborative writing project together?"

"Of that, I have no clue. When it comes to my dad's projects, he doesn't like to tell anyone of them until the time is right. And that is usually when the publishing company, along with his literary agent, are ready to release press releases. I prefer to stay out of it."

"I see. Look, I have to run before I'm late for class. How about a latte afterward? I'm free at 11 a.m." Marc asked.

"Me too. I guess we both have a two-hour lecture ahead of us."

"Yup. How about The Bear's Claw over at the Head of Dean Hall?"

"Perfect. I don't think driving is going to be a good idea in a couple of hours."

"No, it is not. They are calling for a foot of snow, and it's going to be wet. Maybe even some sleet."

"Good choice then. Meet you there."

Gaea watched as Marc turned and headed toward the Bryant Sciences Building. She smiled and made her own way toward a three-story building that housed Shibles Hall.

Bill Pender looked out over the Atlantic Ocean through the double French doors that made up a portion of the east wall of Shaw Manor's widow watch. Some years before, when he purchased the estate, he claimed the space as his personal office and dubbed it his dreamer's hideaway. The space had provided him with solace and the ideal place to write and weave his tales, which had amounted to twenty-one bestselling novels and seven films, with another picture in the making.

He watched as snow fell and swirled, covering the balcony adorning the tower's exterior wall, which housed the widow's watch.

"Winter is at hand," he mused, scratching his graying goatee. Bill couldn't help but think of his two children, who were at school. His nerves came to life for a moment in worry. He dismissed the feeling quickly. Gaea and Vicky were young adult women and fully capable of taking care of themselves.

He walked to his desk and picked up the handset. He pressed a single digit on the phone's pad and listened to it ring. A moment later, a woman's voice came on.

"Mr. Pender?" The head housekeeper asked.

"Is Aerin home yet?"

"No sir, but the radio is saying that the children are being dismissed from school early due to the oncoming storm. Your wife called as well and is leaving work. She is picking up the boy. Hasn't she called you?"

"Not yet. I'll call her myself."

"Very good, sir. Anything else?"

"No. That will be all, Mrs. Douglas.

The Scottish woman had been brought on by Bill and Cathy before their son was born. She had led in overseeing the manor as well as the children for years. Along with two housemaids, the day-to-day chores of the home were well met. One of the housemaids had left to pursue a nursing degree; however, Karen had stayed. After going through several replacements, a young girl of twenty had joined the staff, and she seemed to fit in well. Laurie was a dropout from Sanford High School due to drugs and alcohol. Her mother had been a prostitute and a Heroin addict who died of an overdose when Laurie was seventeen. The girl had gone to live with an abusive uncle and fell into the same rut as her mother. Then, she dropped out of school and was arrested several times. A lenient judge had taken pity on the girl, and through forced rehab, parole, and a short stint at a halfway house, she was able to pull her life together somewhat. The Penders had saved her life, and she was grateful.

It was the same case worker who had managed Vicky's case who brought Laurie to the Penders, not for adoption but for a job and a place to call home. Mrs. Sevigny knew the Penders had a soft spot for hard luck cases, and with Mrs. Douglas as her Boss and an older girl as her co-worker, it made perfect sense. The estate needed a new housemaid.

The arrangement had turned out to be a perfect solution for both parties. Laurie had slid into her duties effortlessly, and even Mrs. Douglas had been impressed with the girl.

Aerin had a strong affection for the girl as well. He seemed to be enamored with her strawberry-colored hair and sharp blue eyes.

Laurie went out of her way to attend to Aerin.

Bill picked up the phone and called his wife.

"Hello?"

"Where are you?" He asked.

"I was about to call you. I picked up Aerin a short time ago and we are just about to leave Luigi's with some pizzas. The snow is not that bad yet, so I thought it was safe to go grab something simple for supper."

"Perfect. I'm sure everyone is hungry or will be, and we don't have to cook. Dammit, I miss Vicky."

"Me too. Be home soon, OK?"

"Drive safe, babe. This is going to get worse."

"I will."

Bill hung up.

The lecture had been enthralling for Gaea, and she had sopped it up like a sponge in a lake, scribbling notes down as quickly as she could. At the start of class, Professor Parkinson returned the quiz from the earlier class to his students. As he handed the result to Gaea, he smiled.

"Perfect as usual, Ms. Pender."

Gaea looked at it, and at the top, A+ was handwritten in gold ink along with a computer-printed grade of 4.0. Parkinson was old school when it came to grading and liked to handwrite the grade on top of the test. A score of D or below was always written in red. Scores of C in orange, green in B and A, and above in Gold. Gaea had always been awarded gold for efforts in his class. The numerical grade was the university's official grade and would be what was recorded. Gaea liked the color and alphabetical grading. It reminded her of grade school.

Marc was nearly falling asleep in his chair, and not because of the subject being taught. He simply knew everything there was to know about cumulus nimbus clouds, and Professor Van Hinkle's endless drawl was boring him to tears.

When the lecture concluded, Marc was relieved that there was no test or quiz in sight. Other than a required brief essay on the subject that he could write in his sleep, he was free to go, and there was a place where he would much rather be.

The Bear's Claw was located in the basement of the Head of Dean Hall. A set of concrete stairs led down to double doors that provided entry to the tavern/café. During the day, the establishment provided made-to-order breakfast, lunch, and dinner, a nice change from the cafeteria food served across the quad. At night, The Bear's Claw became a tavern that hosted live bands, some of which were made up of students studying music as well as spirits, beer, and wine. Two wooden posts were outside of the doors, and signs hung on each. One displayed the bar's logo, which consisted of a black bear's paw, and the other the school's logo, along with a secondary sign that hung below it with the hours of operation. A tripod sign stood next to it with the handwritten specials of the day and their prices. Another notice was posted on the window that read *21 and older after 8 PM. No exceptions other than employees and performers.*

Gaea abhorred the university's Cafeteria and was thankful that her parents had given permission to use her credit card to eat where she wished. Thus, The Bear's Claw had become a favorite destination to dine. The food was nowhere near that of her sisters but far better than the aforementioned slop served on a tin tray.

She entered the passage that served as a mud room. She shook off the snow and stomped her feet to rid herself of it. She passed through a second set of wooden oak doors into the tavern.

Windows lined one side, but were small, as most basements were. Snow had piled up against them, blocking what light was outside. Ceiling lights, however, took over where exterior lighting could not. Dimmers kept the ambient lighting at a pleasurable brightness no matter what hour of the day.

Breakfast was turning to lunch, and servers were running about taking care of the patrons who chose to shelter from the elements outside. Students and teachers made up the majority of the fifty or so patrons. The tavern was large and had an occupancy of nearly 200.

The Bear's Claw was eclectic, and on this particular day, the music selection was from the late sixties, and Bob Dylan was croaking out an old tune that Gaea did not recognize. The tavern itself was decorated as anyone from Maine might expect to find. Various animal heads adorned the walls, along with two bear skins that hung on the walls. A large moose head hung over the entry door, and the required jackalope behind the bar flanked one wall. Booth seating lined the wall where the snow-covered windows were, and a combination of tall two-seaters and larger lower four-seat tables filled up the majority of the space. A fireplace adorned the wall to the left of the entrance. A hallway led back to the restrooms and further on to the kitchen. To the left of the hall was the stage that could accommodate a band, although it was challenged for space.

Gaea looked over and walked toward her favorite booth. As her eyes adjusted to the light, she could see Marc stand up to greet her. He kissed her, and they both sat down.

"So, how did it go?" He asked.

"Fabulous. I always learn so much," She answered. "How about you?"

"Boring as hell. That man drones on like a broken record. I will never understand how he became a professor."

Gaea laughed but then became somber as she looked across the room.

"You see another one, don't you?" Marc asked.

She had told him three years ago about her gift, and he had bought hook, line, and sinker into it. He knew nothing about the paranormal and had never experienced such phenomena. However, he loved Gaea and believed in her completely.

"Who is it?" He asked.

"I don't know. It's a girl our age who is practically begging to come over here. So sad."

"You're using the charismatic thing, aren't you?"

"Yes."

"You can't help every dead person, Gaea."

"I know."

The spirit vanished as the waitress walked up.

"Hey, you two, what can I get for you."

"Two lattes, please," Marc answered.

"And hot!" Gaea exclaimed.

Vicky boarded the Air France flight that would return her to Boston, and then a rental car that she would drive home. She had not told any of her family members that she had graduated early. That would be her surprise. Nearly half a year early, she would be home for Christmas. She had picked up quickly on all of the curriculum and proved herself beyond the expectations of her teachers, who were, in their own right, accomplished chefs. She was natural in the culinary arts, and she passed easily even in the business courses she had taken. Vicky was ready to open her restaurant, but the question was where? Her first thought was New York City, which was where the famous chefs were, and that appealed to her. Now, she questioned that. Her thoughts were that being famous was not as important as family and friends. She had missed all of them, and the brief visits home had proven to be not enough. Increasingly, she was considering a quaint restaurant in Bar Harbor.

She sighed and sank back into her seat as the jet taxied toward the runway.

CHAPTER 2
A New Friend

Himiko Aoki left Knox Hall and walked the short distance to the newly renovated Androscoggin Hall, her bags in tow. The plumbing problem that had plagued the female floor of the dormitory had become unbearable, and her plea to the administration had finally been heard and acted upon. She had been given a new shared room with another girl she had yet to meet. When it came to pairing students together, it appeared to her that it was a random choice at best. Still, she was happy to be out of the situation that had become intolerable for well over a month. With the key in hand, she pulled her luggage up the stairs to the third floor and looked for room 307 B.

Himiko was from Southern California, and she was a third-year undergraduate student studying Astronomy. Her black hair and dark eyes had attracted the male students on campus, but she had no need for such attention. Her focus was on her studies, and she had no friends at the school. That was about to change.

She used her key and unlocked the door, stepping into a common room. It was as large as her previous room but contained no beds. Instead, there were two chairs and a sofa, along with a TV and a coffee table. Artwork decorated the walls, and potted plants were placed tastefully throughout the room. As Himiko looked around, she saw two closed doors to her left and one to her right. Opening one closest to her on the left, she found a spacious bathroom, again decorated nicely and, to her relief, did not smell of sewage.

The other door next to it revealed a bedroom that was occupied by her new roommate. The other was an empty bedroom. Except for a bed, a desk that had a lumbar chair pushed up to it, and a dresser that sat against one wall. A bookshelf adorned the opposite wall. Himiko pulled her luggage into the room and sat on the bed facing a large window that looked toward the quad area of the campus. Snow was starting to fall, and she thought it looked beautiful as it clung to the trees outside of the window. She started to unpack, then changed her mind. Pulling her winter coat around her, she headed off to The Bear's Claw for a hot cup of tea.

Air France flight 1616 arrived at Logan International Airport on time, to Vicky's relief. The forecast called for snow, and a winter storm warning had been issued for Boston that extended up to northern Maine. Vicky was hoping that she could pick up the rental car and be home before the storm hit.

By the time she had retrieved her luggage, found the right bus, and ridden to the rental car center, two hours had passed. It took another hour standing in line to do the paperwork and walk to the compact car she had rented. Leaving the center, she made a wrong turn and found herself driving through tunnels deeper into the city. Another hour passed until she entered I-95 and was finally on her way home. Snow was beginning to fall, and she still had a two-and-a-half-hour drive home.

Approaching the New Hampshire state line, the snow was now falling heavily. Vicky could see fairly well, and up ahead, the blue and red lights of emergency vehicles flashed. Two trucks blocked all but one lane of the highway. A tractor-trailer had flipped onto its side and hit a second truck, causing it to veer and crash into a bus. A Massachusetts State Trooper sat perpendicular to the crash, and a fire department ladder truck and an ambulance were also on the scene.

Approaching the crash, she could see a police officer directing the traffic and lit flares leading to the open lane. Vicky winced and prayed she could make it through the funneling traffic that fought to get by the accident.

"Perfect," Vicky said aloud.

With the snow piling up outside, the students at the university were arriving at The Bear's Claw, and it had filled to near capacity. Most of the buildings on campus had a shared intercom system that was used to keep students and faculty informed of events. The announcement had come that all classes had been canceled for the rest of the day and the following day as well. Most cheered the news, but Gaea hated the lapse in her studies. She knew that the missed classes would be made up, but still it was an unwanted interruption. At least for her, it was.

Marc, on the other hand, was overjoyed. The man was a genius, and his classes were a bore. Still, he plowed through each one, barely able to keep awake most of the time due to the endless dribble that came out of his professor's mouth. When the quizzes, tests, and exams did come, he aced them all, and his grade point average was always 4.0. He suspected that he might be in line to graduate valedictorian in his school of studies. Not that it mattered to him, as he wasn't much interested in personal acclaim. For the here and now, he was seated across from the person who meant the most to him.

Marc reached across the table and took Gaea's hand. "Latte up to your standards?"

"Always, well, except for my sisters."

"Vicky."

"Yes. You have had the pleasure of sitting down to a meal that she created. She is so talented. She is finishing up culinary school this year in Paris."

"Yes," Marc replied, smiling. "She chose well."

"I can't wait to see her again. A couple of times a year is not enough."

"I can imagine," he said quietly.

"She had chosen to study and work in France to gain experience, so neither my family nor I have seen her much in almost four years."

Marc was momentarily distracted by an Asian girl who came into the tavern. She had slipped on the snow-covered entryway and nearly fallen.

"Do you know her?" Marc asked, motioning towards the door."

Gaea turned and glanced. "No. I've never seen her before."

Marc stood up, walked over to the girl, and helped her regain her balance.

"Thank you," The girl said, looking up at the boy. "I don't think I will ever get used to the winters in Maine. "There's not much room to sit in here, it seems. I wanted a cup of hot tea."

"Come sit with us." Marc offered, motioning to the booth where Gaea sat.

"I wouldn't want to intrude."

"You're not. Come."

Gaea watched as Marc led the girl toward her. "Hi. Can you sit with us?" she asked.

"Thanks! This place is packed."

"It's the storm." Marc sat next to Gaea, offering his seat to the girl.

"It's been a busy day. I was barely able to move out of Knox Hall and get my stuff over to the Androscoggin dorm. Knox really needs to be fixed. I'm Himiko. Himiko Aoki."

"Cool. I'm Marc, and she is Gaea. We both live in Androscoggin," Marc said, taking a sip of his latte.

A waitress arrived, and the three ordered drinks. Gaea ordered hot chocolate, Marc a glass of red wine, and their new guest ordered hot tea. The young woman smiled and scurried off.

"I know the problems over at Knox. I would not want to live in it. I hear the place is falling apart."

"It is," Himiko answered. "I haven't unpacked yet. I went into the room, and it was beautiful. Whomever my new roomie is has great taste."

'What room is it?" Gaea asked.

"307B"

Gaea and Marc broke out into laughter.

"Is something wrong?" Himiko asked concerned.

"Not at all," Marc replied. "You are Gaea's roommate."

"Let's order some food to celebrate," Gaea said, smiling broadly. "I was wondering when I would get a roomie, and it seems I have a nice one."

"How about nachos?" Marc asked. "My treat."

"I'm in!" Himiko was simply beaming.

Vicky had finally made it to the Maine border, and it was getting dark. The snow had not subsided, but she was determined to get home. Luckily, the storm had not gotten to the point to which it became a whiteout. Although she had to drive slowly, she was able to make progress and was relieved to see the exit that would take her to US-RT1 and lead her toward home. She still had a few miles to drive, and she hoped that the roads would stay relatively clear.

As Vicky's car ground to a halt for the umpteenth time, her cell phone rang. Glancing at it, she answered, "Hi, Grandpa."

"Are you home yet?" Bob Pepper asked.

Robert F. Pepper was a retired publishing house mogul who had relocated from the City of New York to Bar Harbor, Maine. Vicky's adopted father was Bill Pender, a world-renowned author and the best-selling author of Pepper & Pepper Publishing. As Bob Pepper and his wife Dottie settled into their life of retirement, they had become enamored with Bill and Cathy's children. Vicky, in particular, had caught the attention of Bob and his wife. The attraction had come not only from the girl's culinary expertise but also because of her past. She had been abused by an alcoholic father, and upon his death, the Penders had adopted her. The girl had been an outcast and lay at the mercy of others. Robert Pepper had a soft spot for the underdog.

"I'm stuck in this storm, and there is a crash. It's snowing harder, but I think I will be okay. There is not much further to go, " she answered.

"Good. I know you are going home first, but I hope you will come up here as soon as you can. I have a special pre-Christmas present for you."

"What did you do now?" She asked.

"Now, now. You know better than that."

"Well, you should not tease me then," Vicky said, suppressing a giggle.

"It's nothing much," Bob replied, watching his wife enter his office. He put his finger to his lips to shush her.

"Right. You are such a liar. Once this storm is done and I get to visit with Mom, Dad, and Aerin, I'll head up. I have lots to tell you and Grandma about the school and graduation."

"I bet you do." Just drive safely.

"I will, and no telling anyone else I am home. No one. Understand?"

"Of course." Bob lied, smiling at his wife. "See you soon, Vicky."

"Love you!" Vicky said and hung up.

"So, what are you scheming now?" Dottie Pepper asked her husband, handing him an open legal-sized envelope. "Property?"

Bob smiled and pulled his wife onto his lap. "You just can't stop opening my mail, can you?"

"Habit." She replied, smiling. "Too many years of being your secretary is a hard thing to get over. You bought a building over in downtown Bar Harbor. Why may I ask, but I do have my suspicions."

Bob sighed and tossed the envelope onto his desk. "Vicky should have been our daughter; you believe that, don't you?"

"Yes, I adore her. She is the child I have always wanted but never had."

"Me too, but she is not. She's not really even the Pender's daughter. You know, the day I retired, I told the lovely woman that I handed the reins of the company to a simple fact that I believe in with all my heart."

"What is that?"

"A person does not have to be blood to be family."

Dottie smiled and kissed her husband. "I love you. Now tell me why you bought the building and why you did not tell me that Vicky is coming home early."

Bob looked up at his wife and smiled.

Gaea, Himiko, and Marc ran across the snow-covered quad toward Androscoggin Hall. The campus had been transformed into a winter wonderland, and laughing, the trio began to make snowballs and throw them at one another. Light polls that were placed throughout the campus were the only thing that marked the pathways that were now covered in a foot of snow, and they were lit, illuminating the snowflakes, creating a faux fairyland.

Winter in Maine brought darkness early. As the three had finished eating, it was only 4 p.m.; however, seeing through the onslaught of snow was becoming difficult.

The three arrived at the front door of the hall, and as Marc opened it, the power went out, leaving them in the dark.

"What was that?" Himiko asked.

"Probably a transformer blew," Marc said. "Let's go up the stairs."

As they made their way up the stairs to the third floor, the battery backup lighting system illuminated the stairs.

"Finally," Gaea said, unlocking the door and letting her friends into the suite.

There was no emergency lighting within the Hall's dorm rooms.

"I don't have any candles," Gaea exclaimed.

"Don't worry. I have lots." Himiko said, heading to her room.

A short time later, the common room was dimly lit by two dozen candles in various colors.

"Why do you have so many candles?" Gaea asked.

"I'm a witch," Himiko answered.

"Where is your broom?" Marc asked jokingly.

"Very funny. My Dad is Japanese, and my mom is American. She practiced the Wiccan way of life."

"Isn't that a satanic thing?" Gaea asked.

"No. We believe in Mother Earth and the balance of all living things to exist in harmony. We don't recognize an organized religion that makes us believe in a God or a Devil. Evil does not exist in a form that is real except for that which is created by human beings in our minds. That is false to me. That is the short answer. There is more to it, of course."

Gaea sat back on the sofa and looked at her new roommate.

CHAPTER 3
A Homecoming

Vicky pulled into Shaw Manor's driveway just before 5 p.m. The small car barely made it up the drive through the snow. Since she did not have a garage remote control, she parked as close to the front door as she could before the vehicle bogged down.

Shaw Manor's lights were on in many of the rooms facing the west side of the property. Security lights attached to the garage came on, filling the snow-covered grounds with light. Vicky climbed out of the car and went to retrieve her bags when the front door opened.

"Who's there?" A woman called out.

"It's me, Mrs. Douglas. Can I get help with these bags?"

"Mr. Pender!" The woman called into the house. Vicky is home!"

Vicky waved at Mrs. Douglas and pulled her bags from the back of the car. Karen ran out to meet her, and after a brief hug, Vicky closed the trunk. Picking up the luggage, the girls hurried through the snow toward the front door.

Her father met her in the foyer and pulled her in for a bear hug. "What are you doing home?"

"Surprise! Where's Mom?"

"On her way home with Aerin. She has pizza from Luigi's."

"Fine with me, I am starving. What a long day."

"I'll take these up to your room, Vicky," Karen said.

"Let me help you, Karen." Mrs. Douglas offered. "It's good to have you home, dear."

"Thanks. We'll talk later, ok, Karen?"

"Sure thing!" Karen answered, and the two women headed for the grand staircase.

"So, you didn't flunk out of school or something, did you?" Bill asked his daughter.

"No, of course not. Let's wait until Mom and Aerin get home, and I'll explain over dinner. Right now, I want to hang this heavy coat up and change."

"I guess I can temper my curiosity. They should be here soon. Go change."

Vicky hugged and kissed her dad, then headed upstairs.

"Bill, we're home!" Cathy called as she shut the door and walked toward the kitchen. Aerin came behind her carrying boxes of pizza. "Whose car is outside in the driveway?"

"Hi, Mom," Vicky said, sipping a freshly brewed cup of coffee.

Cathy stopped for a moment and then rushed to hug her daughter. "You're home!"

"Careful, you'll spill my coffee!" Vicky exclaimed, laughing.

Bill leaned against the kitchen counter and looked at them, smiling.

Aerin charged forward to hug his sister. "I'm so glad you're home."

"Me too. Let's eat!" Gaea exclaimed.

The pizza party was held in the dining room with paper plates and plastic silverware. When Vicky and Gaea left for school, the Penders chose to keep their loyal housekeeping staff, and it had become a custom that they often dined with the family for the evening meal. Vicky had stumped for it when she was but a teenager, and after the incident with Belphegor, Bill and Cathy had acquiesced. Mrs. Douglas and Karen had been with the family for a long time, and both Cathy and Bill considered them family members. The addition of Laurie Bennett to the staff didn't change. She was welcomed warmly. Unless the staff was needed for certain affairs, which was seldom, they dined with the family, cleaning up afterward.

"Are you going to tell us or not?" Bill asked, wiping his chin with a napkin.

"OK," Vicky said, smiling. "I graduated early, so I am home for good."

"Yay!" Aerin exclaimed. "So, you are never going away again?"

"I'm not saying that, Aerin." Vicky smiled. "But I have decided to open a restaurant here in Maine."

Cathy simply beamed. "No New York?"

"Nope. I'm not sure where yet, but I want to stay closer to home."

"I've not even had anything that Vicky has cooked," Laurie said.

"You will. I plan on cooking dinner for my entire family, " Vicky said. I would like Grandpa and Grandma to come, but that's not going to happen."

"Why?" Bill asked, reaching down to give Piddles a piece of his leftovers.

The Boxer was starting to show his age as the dog's muzzle was turning white. Piddles gummed the offering gently, dropped the morsel onto the floor, and ate it.

"I guess you haven't talked to them as much as I have. Grandma is not doing so well. Her arthritis is keeping her at home, especially in this weather."

Bill glanced toward the window and watched as the snow piled up on the sill. "Bob is not the most open man in the world, honey."

"He is to me. I'm going up there after this storm."

Bill's phone rang, and he answered it. "Pender."

"Hey Bill, did Vicky get home safely? The missus and I were worried."

"How did you know she was coming home, Bob?" Bill asked, eyeing his daughter.

"Come on, Bill. It was a backup plan for her surprise, just in case."

"Well, it certainly was a surprise for us. How are things up there?"

"Oh, fair to middling."

"We are just finishing supper here. Vicky says she will call you soon."

Vicky nodded.

Bill hung up and frowned. "Really?"

Cathy frowned as well and looked at her daughter.

"We will start cleaning up." Mrs. Douglas said, standing. "Girls, please help."

Karen and Laurie stood up and began to collect the paper plates.

Karen leaned over and whispered into Vicky's ear. "You're in trouble." She giggled.

"Mom, Dad." Vicky pleaded. "It was a surprise, but what if something happened? You always told me to hope for the best and plan for the worst. Just look outside."

"True," Bill said. "But sometimes I think you think that Bob is your father and not me."

Cathy looked at her husband. "Don't be a jerk and stop pouting."

"Dad is a jerk, and I am going to watch TV," Aerin said, pushing away from the table.

"Why does that seem familiar?" Bill said to his wife.

"You earned the title."

Gaea kissed Marc on his cheek as he left her room. Although Androscoggin Hall was co-ed, the dean of the building had a rule that prohibited students from being in rooms of the opposite sex after midnight. Although the rule was antiquated, some of the students adhered to it, but not many. Marc kissed Gaea and promised to see her in the morning. It was not the building rule he was following but the wishes of those he considered to be the love of his life.

"So," Gaea asked, sitting on the couch next to her new roommate. "Tell me why you are a witch."

Himiko looked at her new friend. "Why do you ask?

"Because I am a psychic medium, and four years ago, I battled a Demon."

Himiko dropped her wine glass on the floor.

"How are you feeling, Dottie?" Bob Pepper asked his wife to sit down on their bed next to him.

"Better she replied, sneezing. I can't shake this cold."

He leaned over and kissed her forehead. "Are you warm enough? This storm is bad."

"We have been through things like this before, Bobby." She said, smiling at her husband. "Did Vicky make it home?"

"Oh yes. Safe and sound."

"You didn't tell her that I am sick, did you?"

"You know I am a horrible liar, but trust me, I did not."

"Thank you." I'll be up and about soon. I miss her."

"So do I, my love. So do I."

"Gaea, demons don't exist," Himiko said, picking up her glass and wiping up the spill. "Are you telling me that they do?"

"My friend died because of one, and then it possessed another. It was terrifying, Himiko."

Gaea stood up and walked to the window. Snow was still falling heavily. The lights flickered and came back on. "Let's hope that lasts."

"Gaea, I am serious about this. If what you are telling me is true…"

"Himiko, Demons do exist, and so does the evil that they represent."

"Wow. This changes everything. What my mom told me a long time ago is true. I did not want to believe that evil witches existed. I'm not a bad person."

"I know you are not. I can feel that. Otherwise, I would not have let you into this room."

"I'm having a hard time with all of this," Himiko said, placing her head in her hands.

"I know we just met, but I'm here for you, OK?" Gaea said, sitting next to Himiko and placing her arm around the girl's shoulders.

The following morning came with a cloudless sky and sunshine that was blinding as it reflected off the fresh snow. The Pender, except for the house staff of Shaw Manor, were awakened by the grounds crew clearing the driveway. A dump truck equipped with a plow, along with three snow blowers, was hard at work, and a few others used shovels and brooms to clear the estate's porch, steps, and walkways. Mrs. Douglas had strict rules of going to bed early and rising, and Karen and Laurie were already busy with morning chores. One of them was then assigned to Laurie to do the monthly cleaning of the attic. She opened the door and flipped the switch on the wall. Bright light filled the space. Bill had fluorescent lights installed after what had occurred years before with the demon. Since then, the house has been quiet and peaceful, to the relief of everyone in the manor. Laurie had only heard what Karen had told her, which was not much. After a brief sweeping of the space, she took her broom and the plastic bag holding the dirt and went back down to the second-story hallway.

"All done?" Karen asked."

"Yep. It's not a big deal." Laurie answered, closing the attic door.

"Good. It's laundry day!" Karen said cheerfully. "I've already brought the linens down, so we just have to wash, iron, and dry."

"Yay," Laurie replied. "My favorite day of the week."

"We could be outside shoveling snow."

"True."

Aerin charged into the kitchen and sat on the island. "What's for breakfast?"

Vicky turned and smiled at her brother. Picking up a plate, she placed it in front of him."

"Yum!" Pancakes, bacon, an egg, and an English muffin!"

She smiled and called up the back stairs. "Breakfast is ready. Everyone who is hungry better get their buts down here before Aerin eats it all!"

Gaea and Himiko dressed and headed out to get some breakfast. Their choice was once again The Bear's Claw, as the establishment had a variety of choices and was the closest option. Over two feet of snow had fallen, and the schools' ground crews were out in force clearing it. Luckily, they had already cleared a path that led toward the tavern. Morning classes had been canceled due to the storm, and most of the students had slept in. All, except for the meteorology students, included one Marc Broussard. When there was a weather event such as a blizzard, some professors took advantage of it. He had gotten up early and was now out in the field of study with his fellow classmates.

"It's too bad that Marc can't join us," Himiko said.

"Yeah. He chose the subject, so, oh well."

"He is really cute. "Himiko added, looking at her new friend. "Boyfriend?"

"I guess so. We are just so busy with school; we don't have much time to spend together."

"That's cool. I had a boyfriend, but it kind of fell apart."

"Why?"

"He didn't like the idea of my moving to Maine from California to go to school. He chose the University of Southern California."

"You were talking about Japan," Gaea said.

"Yeah, my dad immigrated to the United States and married my mother in California. I grew up in Los Angeles."

"So why UMO?"

"I felt it was time to start experiencing the rest of the states. When I decide to do something, I tend to go a bit extreme. When I was looking for a school, I couldn't take my eyes off the scenery of Maine. It seemed like a friendly country sort of place."

"It is," Gaea replied.

"Here we are!" Himiko announced, opening the door to The Bear's Claw.

As the two girls ate a couple of stacks of pancakes, Gaea glanced over and saw the spirit of a girl leaning against the wall. She was beckoning her with a finger.

"Can you excuse me for a moment?"

"Sure," Himiko replied.

Gaea wiped her mouth with a napkin and stood, walking toward the apparition.

"Who are you?" Gaea asked.

The girl seemed to be Gaea's age and had blonde hair, but her eyes were non-descript and seemed devoid of life.

"You use the block."

Gaea thought for a moment. "The Charismatic Shield, yes."

"Why?"

"The dead constantly bother me."

"I am not here to bother you." The spirit whispered.

"What then?"

To warn. Beware of the Night Witch."

Before Gaea could respond, the spirit turned and passed through the wall.

"You OK?" A waitress asked.

"I'm fine. Just mumbling to myself about school."

"I'm all about that." The girl answered and walked away.

Gaea returned to the table and sat down.

"Do you always talk to walls?" Himiko asked, giggling.

Gaea looked at Himiko. "Do you know anything about a Night Witch?"

Himiko dropped her fork onto her plate.

CHAPTER 4
The Pepper's

Vicky had been home for nearly a week and was itching to go to Bar Harbor to see her adopted grandparents. A side trip to UMO to see her sister was in order, as it had been too long since she had seen Gaea.

Bill had seen to keeping her Jeep in good running order. The vehicle had less than 20,000 miles on it, even though it was four years old. Living and studying overseas had kept the Jeep in like-new condition. Being parked in the garage was a plus. It had not been seen but one winter, and during that period of time, it was sheltered. To say that it had been pampered would not be an overstatement.

Vicky was ecstatic to sit behind the wheel once again as she headed off to buy groceries up in Wells. She needed supplies for both Shaw Manor and for her visit to the Peppers. Her mom and dad had left her own kitchen ill-stocked, and what was there was not healthy, and Vicky disapproved of the pantry, especially. How could things go to crap so quickly? She had no idea. It had only been a few months since I had been home and had restocked everything. It seemed to Vicky that unless she was there, the kitchen was just not kept up to par.

"Vicky wasn't happy with the kitchen again," Cathy informed her head housekeeper.

"I know Mrs. Pender." Mrs. Douglas answered. "I am not taking the blame for it either. I have asked the girl time and time again to leave a list, and I would see to it being filled. Sometimes that lass can be frustrating!"

Cathy sipped her coffee and laughed. "I'm not blaming you. We all know how she is when it comes to her sacred kitchen."

"A much ado about nothing if you ask me. I have served the manor for many years, and you know that I take all my duties seriously."

"Of course you do," Cathy said, smiling. "You are not at fault. I will speak to my daughter about the lists, OK?"

"That would be much appreciated. I am not a young woman anymore, and I don't take kindly to stressful situations."

Cathy smiled again as Bill walked into the kitchen.

"Who is in trouble now?" He asked, pouring himself a cup of coffee.

"Mrs. Douglas was telling me that you are leaving your dirty underwear on the bathroom floor again," Cathy said slyly.

"Now, that is a lie. I leave them on the bed."

Mrs. Douglas harrumphed and left, walking up the back stairs.

Bill hugged his wife, and they broke out laughing.

Dottie Pepper was feeling better as she sat in her dining room, sipping on soup. The call from Vicky telling her that she was coming up for a visit had rejuvenated the 75-year-old woman. The cold that she had been suffering from had turned into the flu. Fortunately, it did not go into her lungs and cause pneumonia. Her husband sat across from her, his face filled with concern.

"Are you sure you should be up and about, Dottie?"

"I'm fit as a fiddle. I can't lie in bed forever. Besides, my granddaughter is coming for a visit, and she will want to make cookies, and I will be damned if I won't help."

'That's my Dottie." Bob said, smiling. "What is the reading this morning?"

She glanced at the device she had clipped to her finger. It read the oxygen level using technology he could not understand, even though he knew what the level should read.

"It's up to 94.6 percent this morning." She replied.

"Not good enough," Bob said, frowning. "It needs to be higher."

"I'm breathing just fine and feel good. I'll take it easy, OK? Until Vicky gets here."

Bob looked skeptically at his wife. "Don't push too hard too soon."

"I'll lie down after breakfast."

"Good," Bob said, getting up. "I'm going to call Bill and see what's going on with Vicky."

"Thank you." His wife answered.

"You were talking to a wall, Gaea." Himiko was concerned.

"I wasn't. It was a spirit. I told you I am a psychic medium and can speak to and see the dead."

"That is what freaked me out."

"So, tell me about a Night Witch?

"My mother told me about Night Witches when I was a child, but I thought they just existed in scary fairy tales, like folklore. When you told me about fighting a demon yesterday, I thought about it all night. I barely slept. And now this?"

"I'm not sure either," Gaea admitted. "Spirits can lie, but I am not sure about this one. This girl is our age and seems sincere and scared. But look, it may be nothing."

Himiko nodded.

Gaea's cell phone rang, and she pulled it from her pocket and answered it. "Hello?"

"Hey!" Gaea answered, winking at Himiko. "Where are you?"

At first, Himiko thought it was Marc. Then she could hear the voice of a girl, although she could not make out the words. She raised her shoulders, questioning silently.

Gaea placed her hand over the phone and mouthed the words, "It's my sister."

Himiko nodded and sat back.

'No way!" Gaea said, pausing as her sister spoke.

"I'm coming up for this weekend. Can you come?"

"Of course, I can and will. I can't believe you graduated early. I knew you could do it. You are the best!"

"Thanks," Vicky replied.

"Hey, can I bring Marc and another friend?" Gaea asked looking at Himiko.

"Of course, you know Grandpa and Grandma love visitors. And I love to cook. I'll be making some special things."

"I am sure you will. See you soon!"

Gaea hung up and looked at her friend. "This is so cool. My sister is coming up to Bar Harbor, and we are invited!"

Marc had been roused out of bed shortly after leaving Gaea and Himiko's dorm room by his roommate, who also studied meteorology.

"C'mon! Professor wants out in the quad ASAP!" Jeff Drummond said, prodding his friend.

A loud rumble occurred outside.

"Is that what I think it is?" Marc asked, sitting up and starting to get dressed.

"Thundersnow!" Jeff exclaimed.

"That's a rare occurrence. Finally, something to be excited about. Let's go!" Marc replied, and pulling on his coat, the two charged out the door.

It took the two a lot of time as they trudged through the accumulating snow, but eventually, they arrived at the center of the quad, where they joined two dozen other students and the Professor.

"Greetings!" The middle-aged man said. Even dressed in a parka that was best suited to the Arctic, his full, graying beard and round spectacles could be seen under a fur-lined hood. "My apologies for rousing you all from your restful slumber. However, tonight is a special night that has not been witnessed in Maine for a very long time."

"Thundersnow!" Marc called out. "I heard the thunder!"

"Indeed! And quite right, Mr. Broussard." Professor Marty Schulman replied.

Lightning flashed to the east, followed by a faint roll of thunder.

"The thunder is so quiet, " a female student remarked. Like the others, her eyes were glued to the skies.

"It's the snow," Marc remarked.

"Correct again, Mr. Broussard. The snow acts as a sound buffer as its overall mass is greater than that of rain.

"It's so beautiful." Another student said.

As the lightning flashed, it created a sparkling effect on the flakes of snow that drifted toward the ground.

"Magical." Another student remarked.

"That it is a rare phenomenon on our planet." The professor continued. We are not gathered here to be in awe of what we are seeing but to analyze it."

"Why can't it be both?" Jeff whispered in Marc's ear.

"It can. That is why we are pursuing our careers."

Jeff nodded and turned his attention back to Professor Schulman.

Students had produced notebooks and were scribbling notes of what their teacher was instructing. To their relief, the impromptu lecture did not last long, and they were dismissed to return to their respective halls. A few lingered to take in Mother Nature's beauty. Most chose to retreat to the warmth of their beds.

"She is on her way, Bob," Bill said into his phone. And yes, I gave it to her, and both Cath and I think it is a wonderful idea. I just hope she doesn't get curious and open it before she gets there."

"Bill, she knows better than that. It is addressed to me, after all."

"True. But you don't know kids like I do."

"On the contrary, my friend. I do. Your kids are my grandchildren, and I have spent years with them and watching them grow up. Even discipline when you and your with were not around."

"I can never argue with you, Bob. You are right."

"When is Robert F. Pepper wrong?" The old man said with a laugh.

"Not often. Now let me go. I have a novel to write."

"Go then, Mr. Busybody."

Bill hung up and sat up in the widow's watch with his latest novel open on the computer. Standing, he walked to the French doors and glanced out over the Atlantic Ocean. Winter was certainly here and had come early. Nearly two feet of snow had piled up on the balcony outside of his Dreamer's Hideaway, and the sun was not melting it. He sighed and sat back at his desk. Bill read over the last couple of pages, making a correction, and then continued to write.

Aerin had put up a fuss about not being allowed to go with Vicky to the Peppers. She had quashed it with the argument that he had to go back to school. A snowstorm didn't halt the educational process forever. In the end, Aerin had given in with a promise from his sister that he could go next time. A partial win was better than a no-win at all, and after a kiss, he wandered off happily.

Vicky was happy and excited to be driving her Jeep again and heading north toward Mt. Desert Island to see her grandparents. It had been months since she had last seen them. The rear of the SUV was packed with food and other gifts she had brought back from France to give to Bob and Dottie.

"She removed her coat before leaving the manor, tossing it onto the passenger seat. An envelope that her father had given her fell onto the floor. Picking it up, she read the front of it. For Robert F. Pepper. The envelope was sealed. Shrugging, she tossed it into the center console, started the Jeep, and headed down the drive toward Bar Harbor.

"Thundersnow! I can't believe it!" Jeff said excitedly as he and Marc returned to their dorm room. "I'm not going to sleep tonight."

"You heard Schulman. The essay is due by Friday, and there are no classes tomorrow. I would expect the library to be open, so let's go to bed."

"Since when do you go to the library?" Jeff asked.

"One in a while, when I really don't know something and want to find out."

"Right. I've known you for four years, and not one has seen you do research in that building."

"So, I prefer the internet." Marc lied. The truth was that he did spend a great deal of time at the research center's library. He did it late at night when no one was around and did it quickly. "I'm tired. Good night."

"Night," Jeff answered, lying back in bed, unable to sleep.

Marc turned onto his side and listened to the soft sound of the thunder roll outside. Three hours later, he was able to drift off.

As Vicky drove through Bar Harbor, it was, for the most part, deserted. A few people were out and about, and only a scarce few businesses were open for business. "The bare necessities for the locals," she said aloud to no one. Still, it was a winter wonderland that sparkled in the sunshine.

She pulled over for a moment as a snowplow drove by, dumping a mixture of salt and sand onto the road. Picking up her cell phone, she called the Peppers.

"Pepper Mansion, "a male voice answered. "Henry, I am at your service. How may I help you?"

"Henry! It's Vicky. I'm twenty minutes away. Can I get help with my bags and the other stuff I brought? It's good to hear your voice."

"Of course, Miss Vicky. The staff will be ready for your arrival."

"Thank you!" Vicky said and hung up.

Vicky drove up and parked her Jeep near the front door of the Pepper Mansion. She was met by the sight of Henry and two of the female house staff, all of whom stood stiff like soldiers ready for review by a commanding officer. She shook her head, turned off the SUV, and climbed out.

She opened the hatch of the Jeep as the three approached.

"You are expected inside, Miss Vicky," Henry said. "We shall manage the bags."

"It's good to see you, too, Henry," Vicky remarked. "Loosen up, will you?"

She wasn't sure, but Vicky thought she saw a slight smile from the older butler. The two girls giggled.

"OK. Take the one luggage bag and the cardboard box to my room and the rest of the paper bags to the kitchen," Vicky directed.

"Very well," Henry said and turned to leave.

"Doesn't he do anything?" Vicky asked the two girls.

They laughed again. One of them smiled broadly. "Not much unless it is answering the phone or delivering a drink."

"It's good to be home, Becky. And you, too, Sara."

"It's great to see you, too! " The two girls answered in unison. The three hugged.

Vicky turned and walked toward the ornate front door of the Pepper Mansion.

CHAPTER 5
A Weekend Reunion Minus One

Friday morning came, and Gaea had her bag back and stood at the front door of her room, waiting for her roommate to join her. After knocking on Himiko's door numerous times and calling, the Asian girl appeared, still dressed in her pajamas.

"I'm not going." She said. "It's a school thing."

Gaea could see that her friend had not slept as her eyes were bloodshot. "Are you sure? You can catch up, and the weekend away will do wonders."

"Next time, 'k? I really have to do this."

Gaea could feel that Himiko was not OK, but also realized that she was pushing her away. For some reason, the girl wanted space. Resigning to defeat, Gaea hugged her roommate and kissed her cheek. "Next time."

Himiko smiled weakly, turned, and went back into her room, closing the door.

"Oh well." Gaea thought to herself and picked up her bag. Marc was waiting in the parking lot, and they had a drive ahead of them.

"No Himiko?" Marc asked taking Gaea's bag.

"She backed out. She says it's a school thing, but I'm not so sure," Gaea replied. She unlocked her Jeep and opened the rear hatch. Marc placed her bag and his backpack into the SUV and closed the door. The two climbed in, and Gaea started the engine.

"School work? Cramming for an exam?" Marc offered.

Gaea turned the heat on and rubbed her hands together. It's still really cold. It takes a minute for the heater to kick on." She said."

"I'm OK."

"I don't know what's going on with Himiko. It seemed like she didn't sleep at all last night, and she was very aloof this morning. I think it is something else. She didn't *feel* right.

As they left the campus, the heater started to warm up the inside of the Jeep.

"Wow. That was quick. My old Camaro would have taken ten minutes for the engine to warm up enough to put out heat.

Gaea checked the time on the Jeep's dashboard. It read 6 AM, and it was still dark. The sun would not rise for another hour. It took 30 minutes to drive through the town of Orono and merge onto the Maine Turnpike heading south.

"I'm hungry," Marc said. Maybe we can stop and get something to eat?"

"We only have an hour to go before we get to my grandparents' place. I was going to surprise you, but she is preparing breakfast for us. I am thinking it will be nothing more than spectacular."

"Forget stopping then, but maybe you could drive a little faster?" He said with a laugh.

"I'm a safe driver," Gaea stated.

"You drive like an old lady. I'm surprised you can see over the steering wheel." He joked.

"Jerk." Gaea reached over and lightly punched his arm.

Himiko had been up reading the entire night, and it had not been schoolwork. Her mother had given her two books before she left for university. The first she had finished reading during the night, and it gave her insight. The 193-page book was simply titled *Demonology*, which went in-depth on the subject. She remembered the demon that Gaea said she had battled, and it would scare even the most powerful witch. Himiko could not imagine a spell that would even threaten such a creature, let alone destroy or banish it.

It was the second book she was nearly halfway through reading when Gaea knocked on her door, terrifying her. *Rudimentary Disciplines of a Night Witch* was a short book as well, but packed with information on the dark side of magic, including a few rudimentary curses and hexes.

Himiko's mother had not given the books to her daughter in an attempt to prod her into dark magic but to warn Himiko that the craft existed and was indeed dangerous. The girl accepted the books but had doubts about what she was being told. Those doubts had begun to crumble since meeting Gaea.

She closed the book. Upset as she was, her tummy was growling. Deciding to take a shower, she headed over to the cafeteria for some breakfast and a cup of tea.

The sun was just starting to peek from the horizon of the Atlantic Ocean as Gaea and Marc drove through Bar Harbor. The sunlight was revealing a winter wonderland that was picture-postcard perfect. The ice and snow sparkled on the trees as well as the quaint buildings that lined Main Street, most of which were closed until spring. The glimpses of the ocean that they were able to see were of calm water that reflected the new day's light like diamonds.

"It seems like forever since I was here with my family on summer vacation. Five years ago." Marc said quietly, lost in his own thoughts.

"C'mon. We're almost there. The mansion is down near the point." Gaea said, smiling at him.

"Mansion?"

Vicky had gotten up early. At 4 AM she was showered and dressed in her smock preparing Petit déjeuner. This simple French breakfast would be light, delicious, and filling. The first order of business was to bake the crusty baguette that would go splendidly with butter and the tangerine marmalade she had made the day before. She had chosen a variety of fresh fruits from the supermarket to go with the meal. mandarin oranges, blueberries, grapes, blackberries, sliced kiwi, and peaches, as well as pomegranate seeds and a sprinkling of cinnamon over the large bowl, would be delightful. The addition of honey just sweetened the pie.

Vicky had chosen a few different cheeses, mostly European, from France, Belgium, and Denmark. She thought a variety of flavors would suit everyone dining.

Fresh croissants were also a must for this breakfast, and she made the dough and cooked them herself. The last addition was the Belgian waffles. Not French, she would argue, but what better to go with the rest of the items on the menu?

Vicky checked her kitchen again. There were three known guests: Bob Dottie, herself, and Gaea, her boyfriend and her new roommate. Including the mansion staff brought the head number to twelve. She had increased that number by three to include unknown incidentals.

The amount of food she cooked should be more than enough, but not a waste. One of the things taught at culinary school was restaurant management, and that included the management of food.

Dottie walked into the kitchen as Vicky was taking the baguette out of the oven.

"Something smells absolutely divine, " the older woman said, sitting at the breakfast bar at the edge of the large kitchen.

"Grandma!" Vicky exclaimed, walking over and hugging Dottie. How are you feeling this morning?"

"Just right as rain."

"You wouldn't fib to me."

Vicky had arrived earlier in the week and had caught up on all of Dottie's health issues. She had made it a point to learn every detail about the woman's health requirements, including doctor recommendations. Dorothy Pepper had claimed that it was all much ado about nothing, but she loved the attention, and being fawned over was not that bad. She would never admit it, however.

"What was your oxygen this morning?"

"I'm just getting ready to take it, " she answered, setting a small bag on the counter and unzipping it. She removed a small plastic device and placed it on her finger, pressing a button. A moment later, Dottie smiled and showed Vicky the results.

"98.6 percent! That is awesome!" Vicky said excitedly.

"Good enough to help in the kitchen?"

"You bet it is!"

Gaea reached out and pressed the intercom button next to the closed double wrought iron gates that led toward the Pepper Mansion.

"Come through, Ms. Gaea." A male voice responded.

"Thank you, Henry!" She responded cheerfully.

Marc watched as the massive gate slowly opened inward. "Really, Gaea?"

"Don't freak out. This is going to be fun!"

Bill wandered over to his wife, who was wiping the breakfast dishes and putting them into the cupboard.

"Want some help?" He asked.

"I'm almost done, but thanks for asking."

Bill kissed his wife on the cheek and poured himself a cup of coffee. Sitting down at the breakfast bar, he looked at her. "How about going up to the Peppers for the weekend?"

Cathy looked over at her husband and smiled. "Gaea is going, isn't she?"

"Maybe I got a call yesterday from a certain University of Maine Student. And maybe she said something about driving over to see Bob and Dottie." Bill said, grinning.

"I would love to!" Cathy went to him and grasped him in an embrace. "When do we leave?"

"The bags are already in the Range Rover, and Aerin is upstairs packing; I'm just wondering why it is taking you so long?"

"Oh, you!" Cathy scolded. "I'll go up and shower and pack a bag."

"Gaea is not supposed to arrive there until tomorrow morning, so I am thinking we can surprise her and the Peppers."

"Perfect plan. Let me go get ready."

Bill kissed her and watched her speed off towards the back stairs.

As Gaea drove up the road that led toward the manor, Marc sat and looked out at the woods that lined the drive. It was not what he had expected, visiting a mansion. He thought he would see neatly manicured hedges and trees that were placed intentionally to beautify the lead-up to the estate. Instead, it was a mass hodgepodge. I mix pine, maple, and spruce trees, among others. There was no rhyme or reason to it all. Such is the way of Mother Nature.

As she drove the Jeep onto the large semi-circular driveway, Marc took in the size of the mansion—it was large. It was not the huge structure that he had expected, but it was still an imposing building.

Standing outside the large front doors stood Henry, a housemaid, and another man in a black suit sporting a Chauffeur's cap. They looked stoic and professional as they waited for Gaea to pull up and stop.

"What the heck?" Gaea asked, looking across the driveway at an SUV that was parked outside of the eight-port garage that sat near the far northern end of the estate. "That is my mom's car."

"Are you sure?" Marc asked, looking at the vehicle.

"This is great! My parents are here!"

Henry opened the passenger side of the Jeep as the Chauffeur walked around and opened the door for Gaea. The housemaid went to the rear of the Jeep, waiting to take the bags.

"Are you sure this is not some ritzy hotel, Gaea?" Marc asked, stepping out of the Jeep.

Gaea popped the SUV's hatch and stepped out, handing the keys to the Chauffeur, who took them and slid them into the driver's seat.

Henry opened the door and let the couple walk into the massive three-story great room. It was almost too much to take in without pausing for a moment. The floors were ornate and of Italian marble. Massive columns rose from the floor to a domed ceiling above all of it in alabaster white. A large grand staircase was built to the north with a hallway next to it. A glass elevator to the southern wall with another hallway way that began next to it. Above, a balcony ran around the great room, then smaller balconies could be seen on the third floor. Toward the far side of the room, multiple doors appeared to open onto a veranda overlooking the Atlantic Ocean. Another large room was to the left near the doors, although Marc could not tell what it was.

"Gaea!" Aerin called, charging out of the south corridor, followed by Bob Pepper.

Vicky came from the kitchen, with Bill, Cathy, and Dottie following close behind. They all met in the center of the room, sharing hugs and kisses—all but Marc. Feeling out of place, he stood back and watched the reunion.

"Surprise!" Bill said, pulling his daughter in for a bear hug."

"I saw Mom's Range Rover parked outside when we pulled up," Gaea said. "Thanks!"

"I'll bring the bags upstairs, Ms. Gaea," Sara said. "Same room, third floor?"

"Yes, please. It's so beautiful."

The hugging had ceased, and Bill stepped forward. "Sara, Marc's bags go to a room on the first floor. I don't trust him around my daughter." He said mockingly. He turned his daughter around, pretending to inspect her. "No cuts, no bruises. You are not pregnant, are you?"

Marc looked miserable.

"Dad!" Gaea exclaimed.

Bill looked at his daughter and then smiled broadly. He turned to Marc and said, "I'm kidding. Come over here, ya big lug. How have you been?" Bill brought the young man in and hugged him.

"Just fine, Mr. Pender."

"Jerk," Gaea said to her father.

He smiled back.

"It's my family's pet name for me," Bill said, shrugging.

"We can all talk over breakfast," Dottie said. "I am sure everyone is hungry?"

"You bet I am!" Marc replied. Gaea will not stop talking about Master Chef Vicky and her food!"

Vicky smiled broadly.

Two hours later, the breakfast feast had ended, and everyone had left the room and wandered throughout the mansion. Aerin, Marc, and Bill had followed Bob into the library while Vicky, Cathy, and Dottie had retreated to the kitchen.

Later that evening, Gaea and Marc chose to spend some time in the third-floor solarium. The domed enclosure had been a favorite place for Gaea since she was young. The plants were tropical, and fruits such as strawberries, bananas, mangos, and numerous others grew abundantly within the room. A rock waterfall had been constructed, and water poured over it into a pool that held Koi.

The glass ceiling afforded an exquisite view of the sky, day or night. This particular night, Marc fell in love with the solarium at first sight and spent the first half hour looking at and through the various telescopes placed throughout it.

"Spectacular." He said, sitting down next to Gaea on one of the decorative benches that were placed strategically throughout the room, each offering a unique view of the garden and sky."

"I know. When I was younger, this was my favorite place in the house. Before I could use the charismatic shield, this was the one place where the dead didn't bother me. I slept up here a few times."

"Why do you think that this place is such a refuge?" Marc asked, taking Gaea's hand.

"I don't know. There is something special here, and the dead won't come."

"I don't pretend to know anything of these things. I'm a scientist, after all. But I believe you will have all of my heart." Marc said, pulling Gaea in and hugging her.

"And I don't expect you to. Just that you believe me is more than enough."

"I love you." He said, looking into her eyes.

Gaea lay in bed, looking out the windows. A full moon illuminated the ocean and sparkled beautifully. She hadn't felt so at peace in a long time. The addition to her life with Marc seemed to be the icing on the cake that was fulfilling her young life. She closed her eyes and drifted off to sleep.

Gaea walked down the dark hallway, fumbling with her keys. The power had been out for hours, and the campus was in darkness. She had no idea what time it was and didn't have a clue other than it was very dark both outside and inside Androscoggin Hall. Finding the right key, she slid it into the lock and opened the door.

Candles lit the room, and an altar stood in one corner. A hooded figure kneeled over it, murmuring as if in a trance.

"Himiko?" Gaea asked, trying the light switch. Only candlelight remained.

She walked toward the figure when it suddenly turned.

Gaea stepped back. It was her roommate, but transfigured into a horrible creature that barely resembled the beautiful girl. Her eyes glowed red, and her flesh was peeling off of her skull, showing the tendons and bone beneath.

"I've come back for you, little whore. You will not escape me again." It growled and rushed at Gaea."

Sitting straight up in bed, Gaea held back a scream. She jumped out of bed and ran down the hall, charging into Marc's room and onto his bed, clutching him.

She pulled him over and peered into his disfigured face.

"I told you, little whore, you will not escape me again."

Gaea screamed and woke, crying hysterically. A few moments later, Marc came into her room, climbed onto her bed, and held her.

"What's wrong, baby?" He asked.

"Nightmare," Gaea replied, sobbing.

"I'm here."

Gaea looked at him, and finding the kind eyes she had become accustomed to, she fell back into his embrace.

"Stay with me tonight, OK?"

"Of course I will." He said and slipped under the covers, cuddling the love of his life.

CHAPTER 6
Himiko

Himiko was not sleeping well, and her waking hours had been spent reading and trying to understand the paranormal, demonology, and the myth of Night Witches. What she had come to realize was that all three existed and were intertwined together in some sort of macabre way she could yet understand. She could grasp the abilities that Gaea had, being able to see and speak to the dead. Those who passed on became energy, kept self-awareness, and were provided with choices. Souls, for lack of a better word. Gaea had convinced her of such, and what she had uncovered in her studies had convinced her. The demonology aspect of it terrified her, but she could understand the possibility of such creatures existing in the world. What she could not wrap her mind around was how a Night Witch fit into the equation. Himiko was a witch, but it was akin to a religion that respected the earth, and through herbs and spells, she believed in helping, not hindering those around her. Gaea and the two books her mother had given her had thrown a wrench into it all.

Himiko put the two books back onto the shelf in her room and looked out through the window. She still needed more information, but was unsure where to find it. The library for her school of study might have books on the subject, but parapsychology and witchcraft were not part of the curriculum, and she presumed that there would be few, if any, books on the subject. Still, she needed to pursue every avenue. The first step was to call her mother, then off to the library, the computer, and the internet.

"That would be so great!" Cathy said. "It's been a long time."

Bill looked on curiously and took a sip of his morning coffee.

"It was good to hear from you, and we will see you next month." Cathy finished her conversation and hung up. "That was my brother Jeff. He's going to be back in our neck of the woods next month and wants to come visit for a few days."

"We haven't seen Jeff Tarpon and a couple of years," Bill remarked.

"Such is the life of a scientific researcher." She said, pouring herself a cup of hot coffee."

"What's brought him back up to Maine?" Bill asked.

"I guess another wreck off the coast somewhere. That is his thing."

"And he is damn good at it."

"He was saying something about one of his ships being back in Bath for some work." Cathy walked over and examined a plate of freshly baked muffins courtesy of Vicky. She grabbed a blueberry bran muffin. "Want half?"

"I want my own. Yum!" Bill said. "Bring me one of those orange cinnamon ones. The glaze she makes is amazing."

"You got it," Cathy replied and placed one onto a small plate.

Marc appeared with Gaea following. Cathy took one look at her daughter and knew something was not right. The girl appeared not to have slept and looked shaken.

"Honey? Are you ok?" Her mother asked, concerned.

"Just a nightmare." She answered.

Aerin walked in with a smile on his face.

"What are you grinning at, Cheshire cat?" His father asked.

"Gaea slept in Marc's room last night." The boy cackled, walking toward the plate of muffins.

"You little rat!" Gaea exclaimed. "It's not what you think, Dad.

Marc looked horrified.

Aerin took a bite of a blueberry muffin and smiled at his sister. "There were funny noises coming from his room."

"I'm going to kill you! Mom, nothing happened! I was afraid and didn't want to sleep by myself."

Bill laughed inwardly as he watched his daughter and her boyfriend have a panic attack. There was no reason for it. The girl was 22 years old, and what she did was her business. Besides, he quite liked the man.

Cathy spoke up. "Aerin, your sister is old enough to do what she wishes, and that means without your permission or criticism, young man. Understand?"

"I guess," Aerin replied, defeated. "Can I have a glass of milk?"

"I'll get it," Marc said and went to the refrigerator. As he opened the door, he stuck his tongue out at Aerin.

"My question is about the nightmare and why it was so bad that you ran from your room?" Cathy asked. "You have never been one to have nightmares."

"It was Belphegor," Aerin said simply.

"What!?" Bill exclaimed, standing up.

"It was just a dream." Gaea tried to reassure everyone. "I don't think it meant anything." She lied.

"Are you sure, Aerin?" Cathy asked her son.

"Well, not really, I guess. Gaea and I have a strong connection; when she gets upset, I can feel it. It's happened a few times while she has been at school. I can see things as if I am looking through her eyes.

"What?" Gaea said. "You can see what I am doing?"

"Sometimes. But only when you are upset or feel afraid. It's not very often. Though. I'm sorry."

"It's not your fault." Gaea knelt and hugged her brother. "It's part of your gift."

"What gift?" Bob Pepper said, entering the kitchen.

"Just a bad dream, Grandpa," Gaea said.

"That will pass, " he said, smiling. He hugged Gaea and said, "Where is Vicky? I'm starving."

"She went to the grocery store," Bill replied.

"I see. Bill, can we talk later in the library?"

"Sure."

"Perfect, I guess I'll make my own tea this morning. Dottie wants some, also. She is dressing and should be down shortly."

"Fresh muffins!" Aerin said, charging to hug Bob."

Himiko had spent most of the night in the library poring through the books she could find and then hitting the internet. Surprisingly, a book stuffed on a dusty shelf in a seldom-used portion of the Shibles Hall Psychology research wing had proved to be the most informative.

The volume was old and held nearly 400 pages of text printed on yellowing paper. The leather binding was severing with age. It had been printed in Falmouth, Maine, in the latter part of the 18th century by an unknown author(s). The title of the book was *Witchcraft*.

Himiko had never seen such a book before, and as she turned it over in her hands, it felt odd, although she could not understand why. She put it down to the book's age.

Its subject matter covered a wide variety of subjects that a witch or warlock would find crucial in dealing with their craft. Numerous descriptions and instructions on rituals, as well as in-depth spells, took up a great deal of the book. Chapter 23 caught Himiko's attention and was titled *Responsibilities and Duties of the Night Witch*.

Intrigued, Himiko began to read.

"So, what did you want to talk about?" Bill asked, plopping down on one of the sofas that occupied the Pepper Mansion Library. "I'm still pissed that you have a bigger library than mine." He laughed.

"Your library has a better view." Robert Pepper reminded his friend.

"True."

Bob took a folder off a desk and handed it to Bill. "Business proposal."

"Really. We have never done business before, well, other than the writing stuff."

"This is not about us, Bill. I've been doing some, well, say I say, exploration and research into real estate."

Bill hesitated a moment before opening the file. "This is about Vicky, isn't it, Bob?"

The old man grinned. "Open it, Bill."

The multipage document was a contract and a proposal knitted seamlessly together. Robert F. Pepper was an expert in business, and Bill was all too aware of this. Bill read the first page and closed the folder.

"I don't really have to read all of this, do I, Bob? Just give it to me straight. I trust you completely."

"Ok. Vicky has made it clear that she does not want to open shop in New York City. She's not really interested in becoming a famous chef. At least not for now."

Bill nodded. "Go on."

She has told me that she wants to start by running a restaurant right here in Bar Harbor."

Bill tapped the folder with his finger. "So, this is a business plan for her?"

"Yes and no," Bob said, walking over and sitting next to Bill.

I have already bought a restaurant here in town. It is fully equipped and seats nearly 300 people. It is three stories, the first is for dining, the second has a piano bar, and the third can be easily converted into a residence for Vicky. She will be close to home, Bill. For both of our families."

"You seem to have my daughter's future somewhat planned out. How will I fit into this?"

"I bought the building so that part of the loan is on me. I want you to fund this project's renovation, restoration, and startup. She is not going to take this as a handout. Thus, the loan papers are two parts. You and me."

"That is a given, Bob. Vicky is too proud to take charity. She is paying her own student loans, for Christ's sake. She wouldn't let me pay for her courses."

"She will take our help with these contracts and loans," Bob said, poking his finger at the file.

"I like it," Bill said. "How do we tell her?"

"We tell her we are going to dinner. She will not be happy about going out, but she will go. When we get to the restaurant, it will be a surprise because the only things there are empty tables and no other patrons."

"You are devious, Bob."

"How do you think I succeeded in life?"

The wintry night brought on an eerie silence to the Maine woods. The full moon cast its own illumination down through the snow-covered pines. The recent snowstorm had dumped over two feet of snow, of which most had been cleared on the campus' pedestrian areas. All but for a forgotten area of the University that had lain dormant for decades. The upper campus consisted of three halls that were once occupied by students. Now, all but one had succumbed to the elements; the one that remained stood impervious to the elements and remained intact, although empty.

Through the dim light, human footprints could be seen marring the pristine snow as they led toward Newton Hall.

CHAPTER 7
Cinnamon Woodfire

Vicky had returned with bags of groceries and was busy in the kitchen putting them away when her father and Grandfather entered the room.

"Hey, you two." She said, smiling. "I was thinking of making something super special for supper."

Bill looked at Bob. He had a facial expression that could be interpreted as 'Here comes the storm'.

Bob walked over and took a cookie from a large jar that sat on the counter. "Actually, we are all going out as a family tonight. Well, to eat."

"What!" Vick exclaimed. "I just went to the store!"

"Honey, the family is taking you out as a present for graduating and all the amazing meals you have made for us," Bill pleaded. Please come with us, or Mom will be very disappointed." Bill lied.

"And so will," Dottie said, wandering in during the conversation.

Vicky pouted for a moment and then gave in. "OK, if it really means that much to everyone. But I get to cook tomorrow night."

Bill breathed a quiet sigh of relief.

"So, where are we going?" Vicky asked.

Bill looked back toward Bob for help.

Himiko did something that she would not normally do. The library did not allow certain books to be checked out due to rarity, condition, and other factors. *Responsibilities and Duties of the Night Witch* was one of those books. The library was on an honor system, and she took advantage of it.

Himiko thought the book had not been touched in decades, so she borrowed it with the intent of returning it when she was able to read and examine it fully. Slipping it into her book bag, she left the library.

As she crossed the quad, the sun had set, and she was hungry. She spent over eight hours researching something not in her curriculum. It was the weekend, and she had nothing pressing as far as her studies were concerned.

The Bear's Claw was empty as it was a Sunday night. Few patrons ate throughout the tavern, as most students were cramming for the next day's class.

Himiko sat at the bench Gaea usually used and rubbed her forehead. She regretted not going with her and Marc to Bar Harbor, but this new issue had affected her. Her mother's advice was nothing new to her: research and read because it was all real.

A young girl approached with a pen and pad in hand. "Hungry?" the girl asked, placing a menu in front of her.

"I know what I want. Green tea and a spring salad, please."

"You got it." The girl said and walked away.

Himiko reached into her bag, pulled the old book out, and laid it on the table. The cover of the book seemed off to her. It didn't seem like leather. She shrugged and opened it to the paper bookmark she had inserted when in the library.

A paragraph caught her attention:

The Night Witch is the servant of the savant, the one who knows all and controls all, and is the master of the night. It is he who commands us to obey and bend his will. We bow to his will and submit as his indentured servant and keeper of the sacred fire.

Himiko was distracted by a figure standing next to her in a hooded robe and looked up.

"You know nothing." The voice of a girl said, then walked toward the door.

Himiko stood up to follow her and ran into the waitress who was delivering her food. Both stumbled, and the food hit the floor. Himiko stood up and apologized.

"I'm sorry. That girl startled me."

"What girl?"

Himiko ran outside.

The cloaked figure had vanished into the night.

Everyone piled into Bob Pepper's limousine, which, twenty minutes later, pulled onto Main Street in downtown Bar Harbor.

"What restaurant is open now?" Vicky asked. "It's winter break, everything is closed."

Bob smiled. "Oh, I'm sure we will find something."

"No reservations?" Vicky questioned. "Then again, why would we need one? There is no one here."

"The locals need to eat, honey," Cathy said.

"I suppose." Her daughter answered.

The limo drove toward the end of the street. Vicky looked out at the side-by-side buildings. Most looked like converted two- and three-story homes that had been turned into various shops with cafés and bars intermixed. All were closed for the season.

During the summer, the street was packed with tourists eager to take in the sights and the beauty of Mt. Desert Island. The combination of the Ocean and the mountains created a picture-perfect postcard scene. Vicky was in it.

The limo pulled up and parked next to Agamont Park, which was covered in a fresh blanket of snow. Vicky looked confused as she looked across the street at the closed buildings.

"Everyone out," Bob said cheerfully. "We're here."

Where is here?" Aerin asked, looking confused like Vicky.

The group climbed out of the Limo, and a cold winter blast of air coming from the water hit them in the face.

"I'll keep the car parked here, Mr. Pepper."

"Thank you, Douglas."

The chauffeur closed the doors and climbed back into the limo.

"Come on, let's get inside before we freeze to death," Bob said and led the way across the street. He stopped in front of a three-story building that had no sign hanging from it.

"Vicky first," Bill said.

She pulled the door handle, and it held fast.

"It's locked." She said.

"Hmm," Bob said, scratching his chin. "Well, only one thing to do." He reached into his coat pocket, retrieved a set of keys, and handed them to Vicky. "Open the door, please. I think it is that fancy gold-looking one."

She slid the key into the lock and turned it. There was a loud click, and she pulled the door open, stepping inside. The rest of the family followed, and Bill closed the door behind him. Bob turned on the lights, illuminating what was indeed a restaurant, although devoid of people. The room was the main dining room, and it appeared to Vicky that it was ready for business. Tables and chairs dotted the space eloquently; perhaps a hundred patrons could sit. A long bar took up a wall across from the main door and was flanked by doors that she recognized as kitchen doors, complete with traditional porthole-style windows.

A large fireplace occupied the wall to the left, and the required Maine moose head hung over the mantle. The wall to the right was filled with pictures and various memorabilia related to the fishing industry of Bar Harbor. A staircase led up to the second floor. Vicky could smell the scent of cinnamon, but couldn't tell where it was emanating from.

"What is all of this? We can't eat at a closed restaurant." Vicky stated.

Gaea giggled.

"OK, seriously, what is going on?" Vicky begged for an answer.

"You think you can have this ready for your grand opening by March?" Bill asked, smiling.

"What?"

"It's yours," Bob said. "I have purchased the building, and your dad is going to fund the needed renovation and whatever else you will need to get this off the ground. It's a loan, mind you. Every business needs to be able to pay for itself, so it will, over time, pay your two loving investors back."

Vicky stood stunned for a minute as she took it all in.

"I can come on weekends to help if there are no exams." Gaea offered.

"I will come as well," Marc added.

Vicky broke into tears and fell against her father, reaching to pull Bob into a hug as well. "I don't know what to say."

"You only have a few months to get this ready, honey," Cathy said, stroking her daughter's hair. "Do you think you can do it?"

"I know I can do it with some help."

"Which you will have," Bob said. I know a few things about running a business."

"So do I." Her mother added.

"Let's look at the rest of the place," Bill said.

Aerin had already wandered off and started to explore.

The kitchen was in good condition and filled with commercial-grade appliances. The space was more than enough to handle multiple food preparation stations and a side room designed for dishwashing. Three dumb waiters were built into the wall where the bar was located on the opposite side. The large wood-burning stove caught Vicky's attention.

"I think the former owners used that to make their pizzas," Bob remarked.

"It can be used for much more," Vicky said. "Let's see what is upstairs.

The second story was as eclectic as the first. A long bar stood directly above the one on the first floor, but instead of a kitchen, the bar curved around into a semicircle with a serving area that provided access for the waitstaff to the dumb waiters.

The fireplace was duplicated, and a piano bar sat near the staircase. The nautical theme, as well as other artwork, made up the décor's menagerie. A door was built into the back wall that led up to the third floor.

Two double French doors led out onto a balcony that could hold a dozen small tables where patrons could sit and have lunch or a drink. The view was spectacular and afforded the option of people-watching, the park across the street, mountains in the distance, and Frenchmen Bay, which was dotted with various boats, both commercial and private.

The third story was not as large do the slanted gabled roof. It was finished and had been used as the office for the restaurant, although it could easily be converted into an apartment. A full bath had already been installed.

"I can live up here," Vicky said, walking to the front of the room and looking out one of the French doors that opened onto a small balcony.

"That was one of the considerations when I was looking," Bob said, walking up behind her. "A young lady needs her own space."

"Thank you, Grandpa," Vicky said, turning and hugging him.

"Any idea what you might call your new place? We need to get it legal." Cathy asked.

Vicky thought for a moment and said, "Cinnamon Woodfire."

"Why that name?" Gaea asked.

"Because of you and Dad. Remember how you named Piddles and Mom named Lick?"

"Yeah. Situations and circumstances can cause things to name themselves." Gaea answered.

"When I entered the restaurant, I smelled cinnamon and saw the wood oven. So, Cinnamon Woodfire."

"I think it is a splendid name," Dottie said.

"Thank you, grandma."

"And I am going to help, too. You will need help in the kitchen, " the older woman said sternly.

"OK." Vicky laughed. "But not full time. This is not the kitchen back home. By the looks of this place at full capacity, it could be 250 diners. That can get hectic."

Dottie thought for a moment. "Perhaps you're right. This is best left to younger folks."

As they drove home with the takeout pizza Bob had pre-ordered, Vicky was ecstatic and nervous about her new venture. There was a lot to do and not much time to do it. Not only did she have to get the restaurant ready, but she also needed new computers for the waitstaff to input orders and equip her office. She wasn't concerned about building the apartment as the restaurant was more important, and she could stay at the Pepper Mansion and drive to work. Banking had to be set up, as well as establishing accounts with vendors to provide not only food but other such necessities as the linens for the tables.

Then there was the marketing aspect. Local advertising would be important, but Bar Harbor was a tourist town. She was hoping her grandfather could help with that. That brought up the need to hire a graphic designer for the logo, letterhead, and fliers she wanted displayed in the local shops and hotels. And she had to hire staff as well as piano players for the upstairs piano bar. There was a mountain of things to consider and accomplish prior to opening the doors for customers at the Cinnamon Woodfire.

The weekend had come to an end, and Gaea and Marc put their bags into her Jeep for the trip home. Both of them had classes on Monday morning, so they chose to drive back Sunday Night. They had said their goodbyes inside the mansion, where it was warm, and were getting ready to leave when Aerin ran out of the house and got up into the SUV.

Gaea rolled down the window. "What's up, Aerin?"

He leaned into the window opening and whispered, "Vicky's restaurant is haunted."

CHAPTER 8
UMO

Himiko returned to her shared dorm room and sat in the living room with the old book opened on her lap. She could not help but to read further into its dark passages. The subject matter fascinated and terrified her. The girl could never have imagined that such people existed to promote and serve evil. Coming to believe in the occult and the existence of beings such as Belphegor had been a shock that she was struggling to understand. She wanted to deny and push such things away, but recent happenstances were starting to cement themselves in her mind; Gaea being a major part of it. Spirits she had always believed in and had experienced them herself in California. Dark shadows darting across a lighted hallway and the odd feeling that she was not alone sometimes led Himiko to believe that hauntings were real.

Growing up under Japanese influence, she was a very spiritual person but did not partake in Christianity, which dominated the population of the US and a large portion of the world. Himiko had been raised as a Buddhist, although loosely. She had not been taught in the strict manner of the religion, as her mother was a witch.

Buddhist sutras teach that there are four types of demons: three internal demons and one that dwells outside of the human body. The internal demons are afflictions, illnesses, and death, which are easily explained through science. The external demon is not part of this world but of a realm not accessible by the living. It was the latter that she was grappling with.

She closed the book and put it in her room, returning with candles she placed around it. She lit them and rolled out a mat in front of the window. A light snow had begun to fall. She turned off the lights and sat down, crossing her legs to meditate.

"What did he mean by the restaurant is haunted? Marc asked halfway through the drive back to the University of Maine, Orono.

"He sensed a spirit in the building." She responded simply.

"That is damn weird and spooky."

"I felt him, too. He was very calm. I think whoever it was likes that Vicky is taking over the place.

"I don't know how you people live with these abilities. It scares the DeJesus out of me."

Gaea had felt the presence of the spirit when at the restaurant, but didn't think much of it. She had become keen over the years to sense when an entity was benign or aggressive. Most were simply not ready to pass over and remained behind for some personal reason. The man she had sensed had tried to communicate, but it was vague at best. Aerin had probably gotten more from the intention of the ghost. Gaea believed it was the previous owner and was having difficulty letting go of the building and the restaurant that had been a part of his family for a very long time. The man had been so kind that she had felt no reason to use the Charismatic Shield.

"I'm so happy that you came with me and that you offered to help Vicky. It means a lot." Gaea said.

"Well, I love you and also your family. Why wouldn't I?"

"You have your own studies to consider."

"I barely have to think to pass these classes."

"Lucky you. It's starting to snow." Gaea said, turning on the windshield wipers. "Are we going to get a break?"

"Yeah," Marc replied. "We might be in for a rough winter."

"You're the weather nerd." She laughed.

"What!?"

"I'm kidding." She said, grinning.

A candle lit one of the windows on the third floor of Newton Hall, although it was too dim to be seen from the main campus. Inside the room, a small fire crackled in the fireplace of what used to be the dormitory's common room. A cloaked figure knelt before it and adjusted a fresh log with a poker, being careful not to create too much flame and smoke.

The old buildings had been part of a student community that was nearly a half-mile from UMO's main campus. Originally built in 1866, they were intended to be a spearhead for the university. Later, when the quad had been designed, it was decided to build so that the school was more accessible to the town of Orono, and expansion choices had proven to be more desirable after alumni donations of land. When new buildings were constructed, as well as athletic areas, new dormitories were built. Lincoln, Wood, and Newton Halls were renovated, designated the upper campus, and granted to doctoral students. As the years wore on and the school grew, Upper Campus had been neglected as funds were funneled toward the newer areas of the university. In the mid-1950s, the three buildings were abandoned and left to the elements. Only one survived the onslaught of the harsh winters and Father Time. Newton Hall had been built of brick, as the two older dormitories were of wood.

The hooded figure stood and then knelt within a pentagram drawn on the floor. Opening a book, a girl's voice began to chant.

Gaea pulled her Jeep into an open parking spot. Luckily, it was close to Androscoggin Hall, so they would not have to walk far. The snowfall had picked up, although not to the extent Marc would consider it a storm, such as Maine had just experienced.

"Are you sure this is not going to be a bad storm?" Gaea said, turning off the engine.

"It's supposed to accumulate to about an inch," Marc replied. "This is your typical snow coming from the Midwest. It's what Maine normally gets this time of year.

She nodded and stepped out of the Jeep. Marc grabbed their bags, and the two walked through the parking lot toward their dormitory. Ahead, they could see Androscoggin Hall, and the rooms were lit up. Gaea frowned and felt her stomach turn to knots. Her room was lit by flickering candlelight.

Marc opened the door that led up a flight of steps to the first-floor hallway. The recent renovation of Androscoggin Hall included the addition of an elevator to help students move into and out of their rooms. The oversized elevator could accommodate furniture and other large items that one might want. The school had come to realize that the basic furniture that was provided in the past did not meet the needs of their new generation of students.

Marc lived on the first floor, so he helped Gaea into the elevator, kissed her, and promised to see her the next day. She felt uncomfortable as the elevator doors closed and watched the indicator blink from G to 2 and then finally to 3. The doors opened, and she stepped into the hallway.

Her room was two-thirds of the way down the hall on the right-hand side. She felt lucky when she was given the third floor and a room facing the quad, and she loved the view.

She stopped in front of her room, putting her ear to the wooden door. Silence. When she tried the doorknob, it was locked. She thought about knocking, but she dismissed the idea. Sliding the key into the lock, she turned it, hearing the light click of the tumblers. Gaea opened the door, and the nightmare became reality.

Candlelight filled the room, and the overhead lights were turned off. A cloaked figure sat in the dim light, seeming to chant, rocking back and forth in front of the window, its back turning toward Gaea. The low murmuring she could hear sent shills down Gaea's back, and her entire body shook. Unable to call out, she reached for the light switch, flipping it on and flooding the room with bright light.

The figure turned, and Gaea breathed a sigh of relief.

"Hi! How was your weekend?" Himiko said, standing up. She was dressed in her pajamas. Pulling the top down from her pink panther hoodie, she crossed the room and hugged her roommate.

"You scared the crap out of me," Gaea said.

"I'm sorry. Normally, I meditate in my room, but you were gone, and the vibe is better in this room, " she explained.

"It's OK. I'm sorry too. I haven't had a roomie for a long time, so it's just adjustment jitters."

"I'll let you know from now on, 'K?

"' K," Gaea said, hugging her new friend.

"Hey, how about heading over to The Bear's Claw for some tea?" Himiko asked.

Gaea looked out the window, and the snow was falling heavily. She pointed out toward the storm.

"Wow, I thought this was supposed to be light?" Himiko stated.

"Me too. Marc said it was going to be just an inch. I guess he is not such a good weatherman after all." Gaea said, laughing.

"Who is?" Himiko laughed with her. "Might as well be guessing the winning lottery numbers."

"Tomorrow morning, breakfast, OK?"

"On me this time. And Gaea?"

"Yeah?"

"Thanks for being my new friend."

Robert Pepper did not know how difficult it was to launch a startup business. In fact, he never had to do it. Pepper & Pepper Publishing had been handed down to him and was well-established when he took the reins. Expansions were not the same as a new business from the ground up. He sat at his desk in his office and rubbed his temples. If it were not for Dottie and Cathy, he realized he would have been completely lost. He could, of course, pull in favor of his old company, but then thought better of the idea. He had severed all ties with it and was happy for doing so. This was a new endeavor, and he could hire new people to help. Bill was also useless in this, except for opening his checkbook and helping fund Vicky's new restaurant. It seemed Bob would be doing the same.

Dottie walked into his office carrying a manila file folder. She kissed her husband's cheek and sat on one of the luxurious chairs that faced his desk.

"I did some preliminary numbers for Cinnamon Woodfire." She said, placing the folder onto Bob's desk.

Bob looked at her. Images of her as his hard-nosed secretary flashed through his mind. Dottie had always been a stickler for details when it came to her duties. The thoughts made him smile. Perhaps this new project was what she needed. For some people, retirement was not all that it was cracked up to be, and she absolutely adored Vicky.

Life had fallen into a day-to-day rut for the couple. They had done their traveling, and at their age, simply going out for dinner was no more than a simple occurrence. Bob had been contemplating ways to spark up their lives, and when Vicky had called him on wanting to open up shop near home, it was more than the flicker of a candle for the old man. It was a bonfire.

"Tell me the bad news," Bob said, sitting back and crossing his arms across his chest.

Dottie opened the folder and smiled. "It's like old times, isn't it?"

Bob turned his head and looked out at the falling snow, trying not to break out laughing. He was feeling something that he had not felt for a very long time. Looking back at his wife, he broke into a wide grin, leaned forward, and kissed her.

"It is, honey, but I think this will be fun."

Dottie frowned. "My preliminary assessment of this is going to cost two and a half million dollars."

"The building cost most of that, and I paid cash for it."

"I know we did." She replied, correcting her husband. "It's all fine. A big chunk of the remainder is marketing. Vicky wants to do a lot for the restaurant, such as upgrades to the kitchen, computers, and other improvements. She is a smart cookie. We all agreed to wait on the renovation of her apartment until next year, which could be close to seventy thousand dollars. I have also looked at the inspection report. The overall building is kind of OK. However, the roof needs to be redone, and the heating system is antiquated. Another forty thousand minimum."

Bob stood up and walked over to look out over the ocean. 'It's snowing harder." He said.

"Bob?"

He thought for a moment. "I read that report, and I think the investment is solid. All of those buildings are old but were built to withstand the test of time. I think it is the perfect fit for Vicky. Did you see how her face lit up?"

"I did, but I left her to the moment."

"She loves you with all of her heart."

"And I do her as well," Dottie said, standing up and walking over to hug her husband. I never thought I would have children, let alone grandchildren, and this one is such a blessing, even though she is not ours."

"But she is, honey. Blood does not define family."

"This is crazy," Gaea said, standing outside on the front steps of Androscoggin Hall. Himiko stood next to her as they both looked out towards the campus. One inch had turned into nearly two feet of snow, and it was blowing into huge drifts created by high winds.

"Where is he?" Himiko asked, pulling her parka over her head.

"Who? Mr. Weatherman?"

"I'm right here," Marc said, coming out through the door. I'll have to check on this. It was not supposed to be this bad."

They could hear the university's ground crew's snow removal machines in the distance, but had yet to clear the walkways from their dormitory to the quad. They had been caught off guard as well.

"It looks like if we are going to eat, we have to walk through this stuff," Himiko said.

"The snow is light, so it will be easy," Marc stated.

"Good. Then you forge the way, Mr. Weatherman, and Himiko, you are off the hook. He is buying breakfast."

CHAPTER 9
The Bear's Claw and Advice

Bill was feeling content as he worked on his novel. It wasn't actually his alone, as he was co-writing it with another novelist. The endeavor was new as he tended to work alone, but the opportunity to collaborate with another well-known author was appealing. Dr. Pickling was a bestselling author of mystery romance stories that dabbled on the border of the macabre. Bill was solid in his genre of spies, espionage, and the secret side of government. The two seemed to be a match made for success. Co-writing a novel also gave more time to both authors, as once they finished a chapter, it was sent off to the other to review and continue the story. The concept was fun and provided a respite from the three thousand words a day Bill demanded of himself. It wasn't simply the words; it was the thought process and the imagination it took to weave the tales. Then, he had to edit what he wrote from the day's work. Dealing with raising children as well as day-to-day problem-solving made for some very long days.

Cathy had welcomed her husband's decision to co-write a novel as well. Her workload had dropped off drastically when she had given responsibility to others. With Vicky's new restaurant a reality, help was needed to get it up and running.

Vicky had gone to her building the first thing in the morning. As she drove toward downtown Bar Harbor, she came up with a wonderful idea that she thought would excite her mom. The new purveyor had made it clear that she did not like the existing décor at the building, so she came up with the idea of using items from Cathy's antiquities shops to enhance the restaurant and also sell them on consignment. Most of the restaurant's clientele would be tourists who would change throughout the season, thus always new eyes on the merchandise. Vicky did expect to eventually attract a local following as well, but displaying the antiques seemed to be a win/win situation for both of them.

Vicky parked, unlocked the front door, and walked into the restaurant. She decided to lean on her training in France and would mix some local dishes with Parisian flair. A large portion of the tourism during the summer came from Canada. The Province of Quebec, in particular, although Canadians in large numbers enjoyed visiting the coast of Maine. She would offer numerous bisques using local Maine seafood as well as a dish called poutine, which was made from potatoes, curd, and a rich, savory gravy that she would hand-make herself. Belgian waffles would also be on the menu, again, her own recipe. The menu would be delicious and diverse.

Vicky wanted the décor of the Cinnamon Wood Fire to complete the restaurant's ambiance, and she believed some antiquities from her mom's shops would do the trick.

She did not want a formal restaurant and preferred a more laid-back atmosphere where people would come to eat and have fun. Thus, the second-story piano bar was a consideration when renovating, although she hadn't quite decided what to do with the space. She was throwing around the idea of getting rid of the piano bar altogether and putting in a proper stage for live music. Not this year, she surmised. She didn't have much time to prepare for the upcoming season, and the restaurant and food were her primary concerns.

Vicky walked up the back stairs and paused before turning on the light. For a brief moment she thought she saw a shadow dart across the room near the window that looked out over the street. Turning on the light there was nothing there. Sitting down at the small desk she turned on her laptop and placed her cell phone next to it. It was time to research vendors.

Mornings at The Bear's Claw tended to be busy as it was the favorite dining spot on campus. It was restricted to students and faculty of the school except for hired staff and performers such as musicians.

Gaea slid into her favorite booth, and Himiko sat next to her. Marc preferred to sit across from Gaea so he could look at her.

"I need to tell you something," Himiko said, opening up the menu that a young waitress had placed in front of her. "I was sitting here the other day when something happened, Gaea. It upset me, and that was why I was meditating when you came home."

Gaea motioned for the waitress to leave. "A few minutes, OK?"

"Sure! Take all the time you need." The young girl answered.

"So, tell me. What's up?" Gaea asked.

Marc looked at the two girls listening intently.

"It was very strange." Himiko started. "Well, first of all, I didn't go with you both because of what you told me about ghosts and demons, Gaea. I am a witch, as you both know."

Gaea nodded and reached out to hold the girl's hand.

"This spirit shit freaks me out," Marc added.

"Are you OK?" Gaea asked Marc.

"Yeah." He answered. "It's all just weird to me. Please go on, Himiko."

"Well, I came in here for supper and sat here like we are doing now. This whole demon thing was freaking me out, as well as Night Witches."

"What is a Night Witch?" Marc asked.

"I didn't believe it, even though my mom told me about them. She had told me that people chose to use witchcraft for evil to harm others and to serve dark spirits. I didn't believe it. I use my witchcraft for the benefit of others and the earth.

"So?" Gaea prodded.

"I think I saw a Night Witch, and she spoke to me."

Vicky spent the day making phone calls, jotting down potential vendors and contractors, and trying to convince her mother to sell antiques and artwork at the new restaurant. The latter was the easiest of chores. Cathy had fallen hook, line, and sinker for the idea and praised her daughter for the prospect. Since all of the restaurants were closed around her, it took time to figure out what food vendors were available. After a few hours, she had finally narrowed it down to the two that provided the best service. Central Maine Fresh Produce and New England Restaurants, LLC. Fresh seafood was available in town and could be acquired easily as needed.

She yawned and closed her laptop. It was beginning to get dark outside, and she still had to drive back to Pepper Mansion. Vicky slipped the computer into its satchel and picked up her phone, heading down the stairs. She paused for a moment to look around the piano bar before retreating down to the main restaurant. She walked through the kitchen, taking a mental note of what needed to be replaced or upgraded before heading toward the front door. Vicky turned the lights off and walked outside, turning to lock the door. The shadow darted across the room. Stepping back into the restaurant, she turned the lights on and called out.

"Hello?"

There was no response, and there was nobody in the room. She closed the door, locked it, and headed for her Jeep.

"What do you mean you saw a Night Witch, and she spoke to you?" Gaea asked.

"This person simply stopped at the booth, didn't even look at me, and said, "You know nothing.""

"Did you see who she was?" Marc asked.

"She was wearing a hooded cloak. I stood up to chase her out the door and ran into a waitress, so by the time I got out there, she was gone."

Recalling the event had made Himiko nervous, and it showed on the girl's face.

"Himiko, we can't know for sure it was a Night Witch," Gaea said.

Marc scratched his head and sat back, signaling for the waitress. "I need some breakfast and stat."

"Yeah, let's eat," Himiko said. I'm sorry to be such a downer."

"It's OK. What are friends for?" Gaea smiled. "I need to go to the restroom. Order me a coffee and the number 7, Marc. Please?"

"You got it."

The lady's room of The Bear's Claw was clean but somewhat atypical for a tavern. It had a tiled floor along with a half dozen stalls that contained toilets. A counter that held three sinks stood beneath a large mirror. Two fake plants tried to brighten the space, but the room smelled clinically clean. Gaea felt as if she were in the bathroom of a hospital.

She washed her hands and then bent over to wash her face. Standing up, the apparition of the girl she had seen in the main dining room stood behind her.

"What do you want?" Gaea asked the apparition.

"It's real." It whispered.

"What is real?"

"The witch."

"How do you know?" Gaea asked.

"She killed me." The ghost answered, then turned and vanished through a closed stall door.

Cathy walked up the spiral staircase and into Dreamer's Hideaway, where her husband was typing away.

"Hey." She said, sitting down on a chair at the head of the stairs.

"Hey," Bill said, taking off his glasses. "What's up?"

"I just got off the phone with Jeff."

"How nice. What's up with your brother?"

Cathy frowned and thought for a moment. "He and Roli want to come visit."

"Cool. Why so concerned?"

"He and Roli got married," Cathy said matter-of-factly.

"We knew of their relationship, and I believed that it was only a matter of time before they came out. I think it's cool."

"I was just thinking about Aerin," Cathy said.

"Honey, with our sons' abilities, do you think he doesn't already know?"

Cathy smiled, stood up, and walked over to hug and kiss her husband. "I guess I am being an old mother, protective hen."

"When are they coming to visit?"

"Later this month, after their honeymoon in Hawaii. They are adding a new ship to their research fleet."

"Perfect. I am sure the kids will be anxious to see Uncle Jeff and Aunt Roli." Bill said, chuckling.

"Don't be a jerk."

"There is that word again."

Gaea sat down next to Marc and looked across the table at Himiko. Marc looked at Gaea with a concerned look on his face.

"What's wrong, babe?" He asked.

"You are right, Himiko."

"Right about what?"

"The Night Witch being real."

Himiko looked stunned. "How…how do you know?"

"The dead girl that appeared to me the other day just came to me in the restroom."

"OK, this is freaking me out again," Marc exclaimed. "What did she say exactly?"

Gaea looked at Marc and then back at Himiko. "She said it's real, and when I asked what was real, she answered the witch. I asked her how she knew, and she said she killed me."

Himiko's face went ashen. "Am I in danger?" She asked.

"I don't know," Gaea answered sincerely. "The ghost turned and left before I could ask her anything else. It did seem to be a warning of sorts."

"Damn creepy," Marc said.

The waitress arrived with plates of piping hot food and placed them one by one in front of the trio.

"Enjoy!" She said cheerfully and walked away.

After Gaea related her experience, none of them felt very much like eating. Marc paid for the meals, and the three left The Bear's Claw.

"So, what do we do now?" Marc asked.

"I, for one, want to know who this dark witch is," Himiko said.

"I agree," Gaea added. "If what this spirit told me is true, there may have been a murder."

"And I don't want to be the next victim." Himiko said concerned. "So where do we start?"

"I have an idea," Marc said, pointing to a device mounted to the side of the building.

"Of course. Surveillance video. She must have been caught on camera!" Himiko exclaimed. "Good thinking!"

"When did you say you saw the witch?" He asked.

"Saturday afternoon. The sun was setting when I walked to The Bear's Claw."

"OK. Let me see if I can pull some strings and get hold of the video. In the meantime, I need to get to class."

Both girls nodded and watched Marc run off across the quad.

"What are you going to do?" Gaea asked.

"Try to find out more about Night Witches and the dark black magic that they use. You?"

"I think I'll make a couple of phone calls. There might be someone who knows something about this dead girl who is haunting me. I think she knows a lot more than she tells me when she appears."

CHAPTER 10
Heart of the Night

Aerin felt guilty about not telling Vicky about what he saw and felt at the restaurant. Confiding in Gaea may not have been enough, as she might not think it was important enough to tell her sister. Gaea had felt the presence of the spirit, but felt that it was benign and of no threat. Aerin had his doubts. He knew a liar when he saw one. This ghost just might be hiding something.

Bill and Cathy didn't think Aerin was old enough for his own cell phone, and the only landline was in the widow's watch. Dad's office was still off-limits, and just going into it without permission was a strict no-no. The boys' dilemma was how to call Vicky and talk to her. He didn't want to alarm his mother or father with another concern about a potentially bad ghost when it might be for naught.

His solution was Karen, the longtime live-in housemaid who had taken to him since he was very young. He certainly did not trust Mrs. Douglas. The head housekeeper would rat him out at the drop of a hat. Asking Karen to use her phone was the solution.

Aerin's excuse came easily enough, and he didn't even have to fib. Hold back some information, but do not outright lie. His mom had gone to one of her shops, and his dad was in his office writing. He told Karen that he wanted to call his sister to talk and had no way to do it. The phone on the kitchen wall had stopped working months ago, and his parents had not bothered to have it replaced. Karen was more than happy to let him use her cell phone.

"Hi, Karen!" Vicky answered cheerfully. "What's up?"

"This is Aerin, sis. I am using Karen's phone."

"What a surprise! How's it going?" She asked.

"I'm OK. I'm calling because I think your new restaurant is haunted."

"What?" Vicky asked, sounding concerned.

"I don't think it is a really bad ghost." Aerin tried to explain.

"What do you mean by not really bad?"

"I'm not sure. I know it was a man, and he looked much older than Dad 'cause he had white hair. He wouldn't talk to me and ran away. I just wanted you to know what I saw."

"Where did you see him?"

"On the third floor."

Vicky dropped her phone.

Gaea's class was coming to an end, and she began to collect her book and class materials when her professor walked to her and dropped a quiz on her desk.

"Another wonderful job, my dear." He said before walking on to the next student.

Gaea had discovered that she had another gift beyond what she already had. She was able to see and speak to the dead, but recently discovered she could sense things about the living. Professor Parkinson was a strange bird, and she could tell that he had thoughts about her, but she could tell that he would never act upon them. He was a nerdy pervert, maybe, but not a criminal.

She picked up her backpack and headed out of the lecture room. She wanted to talk to Marc.

Vicky was unhappy as she sat in her office on the third floor of Cinnamon and Woodfire. The telephone call from her younger brother was upsetting. She had been in the process of calling and setting up appointments with contractors to get estimates for the work she wanted done in the restaurant. The restrooms were in dire need of renovation.

She turned and looked across the room that she hoped would become her office and apartment. Currently, it was a little more than a wide-open space except for a bathroom.

"I know you are here, " she called out. My brother and sister are psychics and saw you. You are an older man with white hair. Show yourself."

The room remained silent.

"Really?" She asked again. "Don't tell me I am being haunted by a cowardly ghost."

Again, there was silence throughout the building.

Vicky gathered her belongings and headed downstairs. She had done enough for the day at the restaurant and could make calls from Pepper Mansion.

"I'm not afraid of you." She called out as she walked down to the first floor. "We beat a demon's ass, so kicking you out of here will be easy. I don't want to if you are nice but don't screw with me. I am here to make this restaurant great again, help the community, and serve the tourists."

Silence.

Vicky locked the door, crossed the street, and climbed into her Jeep. She didn't hear the crashing of the pots and pans hitting the floor in the kitchen.

"Anything?" Gaea asked that afternoon as they sat at The Bear's Claw.

"It's going to be a couple of days. My contact over at the campus police department has access to the videos but needs time to dig through the database and compile it. He told me that all CCTV surveillance cameras on campus flow back to the police station. It is watched periodically, but a girl leaving The Bear's Claw wouldn't raise any suspicion."

"I can understand that. People come in and out of here constantly, and its winter. A cloaked girl would be nothing out of the ordinary."

"It wouldn't. Where is Himiko?"

Gaea sat back on the bench and looked out the window. "She should be here soon. She went to the library after class. Look, it's snowing again. Forecast, Mr. Weatherman?"

"I'm switching to Vulcanism. Screw trying to predict this crap." He said, grinning. "Volcanoes are more predictable."

"And you think that will be easier to forecast?" She said, leaning over the table to kiss him.

"No, but they are warmer." He said, returning the kiss.

Himiko had a headache. Her class had bored the hell out of her, and it didn't help that she was distracted by recent events. She was glad when it was over. She then went to the library and tried to do more research, but she had exhausted the few things they had on witchcraft and the occult. She had not learned much more and was at a dead end. Her relief was going to The Bear's Claw to meet her friends.

As Himiko left the library, the snow was falling harder, but had yet to accumulate to the point where it was difficult to walk through it. She couldn't help wondering if it was going to snow every day this winter. She pulled her scarf tighter around her neck and started the two-hundred-yard trek towards The Bear's Claw.

Nearing the tavern, something caught her eye. To the north side of the quad, an unused road cut its way up through the dense woods. It was not plowed and was impassable to vehicles except a snowcat or snowmobile this time of year. Himiko squinted through the intensifying snowfall and, for a moment, thought she saw a person making their way up the road along the tree line. She looked again and saw nothing. She shrugged and entered The Bear's Claw.

"There she is," Gaea said and stood up to hug and greet her friend. Marc exchanged hugs with Himiko as well, and the three sat.

They ordered and ate while watching a trio of musicians set up on the stage. By the look of the set, Marc surmised that it was a jazz or blues group. An upright bass, along with a keyboard player with another on saxophone, was more than a clue.

"You guys want to stay and watch the band for a bit?" He asked the girls as a young waiter cleared their plates.

"That would be wonderful. I could use a nice distraction." Gaea answered. How about you, Himiko?"

"I'm in. After the last few days, I could use a break as well. Class today bored the crap out of me."

Marc laughed. "Tell me about it. I nearly fell asleep in mine. If it wasn't for that goofy Professor Schulman, I might have. He is such a trip."

"My abnormal psych professor is also a bit off," Gaea added. "He thinks naughty things about me, but I don't think he is dangerous."

"How do you know that?" Marc asked.

"It's this new ability I seem to have. It is not as strong as being able to see and speak to the dead, but I can feel it getting stronger."

"What is it?" Himiko asked.

"Well, it's weird. I can feel what someone is thinking, but not exactly what. It is almost like I can tell what kind of thoughts they are having. Does that make any sense?"

"Wait," Marc said, "So if I were to tell you that I was actually from Texas, knowing it was a blatant lie."

"I think I would be able to tell that you were lying to me."

"I think I might need you to teach me this charismatic shield thing." He said, grinning.

"Not on your life." Gaea smiled.

"So that is how you knew to trust me when we first met," Himiko stated.

"I could feel that you were a good person, and your thoughts just resonated with goodness to me. Like I said, I don't know what you were thinking, and I hope I never get that ability. Getting bombarded by everyone's thoughts would drive me mad. I would never be able to drop my shield."

Marc reached across the table and took Gaea's hand. "I will never lie to you."

"Liar." She said, smiling.

"Perfect. I am so screwed."

The waiter showed up with their bill.

"My turn," Himiko said, taking it.

"If you want anything else, I can take the order, but a new server will start shortly. The bar is opening up."

"Sure. How about a pitcher of beer?" Gaea asked.

"Sounds good to me," Marc added.

"I'm only twenty," Himiko said sadly.

"I'll bring an extra empty water glass. But don't tell anyone. You three don't seem to be the sort to get rowdy and tear the place up." He said, smiling at Himiko.

"Thank you." She said and turned back to her friends. "Looks like I'm in too."

It didn't take long before Aerin broke down and went to his mother to confess that he had called Vicky and told her about the haunting of her restaurant. To his surprise, she didn't take it hard. In fact, she almost blew it off as just another odd happenstance that occurred within the Pender family. With one sensitive being herself as well as two psychic mediums in Aerin and Gaea, she was amazed that the dead from all over Southern Maine were not standing outside of Shaw Manor waiting for an audience. Ghosts did not bother her. Demons were terrifying.

The band was well into their first set when Gaea's phone rang.

"I had better take this. It's my mom," she shouted over the music. Standing, she pulled on her coat and ran out the front door. Outside the tavern was not much better than inside. The wind had picked up and was howling, blowing the snow into drifts across the quad.

"Hi, Mom. Is everything OK?" She said into her cell phone.

"I don't think anything serious. Aerin just told me about the ghost in Vicky's restaurant."

"Oh yeah. I felt that it was an old man and nothing malicious. He might have owned the building in the past or maybe the restaurant. It felt to me that he was being protective of it."

"Can you call Vicky and talk to her? I don't want her getting crazy over this for no reason."

"Sure. I was thinking of heading over to the island this weekend and bringing Marc and my new roommate."

"You have a new roommate?" Cathy asked. "You didn't tell me."

"Oh, she is really sweet. Her name is Himiko, and she is a witch."

Cathy almost dropped the phone. "A witch?"

"She's a good one, Mom. Nature, herbs, and such. Don't get in a tizzy. Trust me, you will love her when you meet her. She is Japanese."

"You know I trust you, Gaea. But being a mom is being a mom. And what is that music that I hear?"

"It's a jazz band here at The Bear's Claw. It's snowing like crazy up here."

Cathy looked out the window, and it was clear. "Must be a local thing because it's not snowing here."

"Good for you. I'll call Vicky, OK?"

"Thank you."

Gaea hung up and went back into the tavern.

Vicky wasn't afraid, she was pissed off. She couldn't sleep, so she drove back to the restaurant, and it was already getting dark. The kitchen was a mess, with pots and pans strewn across the room. As she picked them up, she couldn't help but call out in anger.

"So what now? I told you I am here to continue on with the restaurant, and you are turning from an old ghost codger into some sort of weird poltergeist? C'mon, really?"

A ladle hanging from a rack rattled gently against a spatula.

An hour and a half later, she locked up and left without incident. Vicky looked through her windshield at the heavy snow that was falling. She put her Jeep into four-wheel drive and headed for Pepper Mansion. The snow had arrived in Bar Harbor, Maine, once again.

CHAPTER 11
Confliction & Confections

Vicky had another concern as she worked to prepare the restaurant for the upcoming season. Taking the winter months off didn't appeal to her. Her love for her craft was too great. Most of the shops around her closed for winter break, and she could see why. No tourists, no money. She reasoned that the restaurant would not do well, but she still had a kitchen.

She was sitting in the mansion's kitchen flipping through a local publication when she came upon a full-page ad that gave her an idea. The Bar Harbor Trader was published weekly and had a slew of various things for sale, a realtor section, and happenings throughout the town. It was the latter that had caught her attention. A local church was having a bake sale for charity, and people were needed to donate their confectioneries.

Vicky had been looking for an excuse to fire up the new kitchen for a test run. Some of the new appliances had been ordered but were not yet available. Still, she had the wood-fired oven and two gas ovens at hand and ready for use. The two industrial gas cooktops were ready and functional as well. She had turned on the large mixing vat as well as other appliances, and all were in proper working order, although everything needed thorough cleaning.

She had nothing in her freezer, coolers, or pantry, so she would have to go to the grocery store for ingredients. Delivery accounts had yet to be set up and would not be needed until the grand opening of Cinnamon and Woodfire.

"Look at this, Grandma," Vicky said excitedly, handing the Trader to her.

Dottie looked over the advertisement and looked up at Vicky. "A bake sale? What are you up to?"

"I want to try out the new kitchen, and what a great way to start getting my cooking out to the people." She said. "Look here, it says that all contributors will be recognized for their work and donation to help the homeless. What do you think?"

"I think we can send staff from here to clean the place. That is no concern. But you will need help in the kitchen."

Vicky thought for a moment. "I think Sara will help. She has helped me in your kitchen a lot of times. She knows how to do things and likes to cook. I was also hoping you would help, Grandma."

"Of course I will. How many things do you plan on cooking?"

"A lot of different things," Vicky said, becoming excited.

"We might need more help. I'm not as spry in the kitchen as I used to be, and then we have to consider cleaning as we go." Dottie reminded her.

"Of course." Vicky thought for a moment. "I know! And it is perfect."

Vicky picked up her phone and made a call.

"Tell me about that road that leads up into the woods," Himiko asked, sipping beer.

The band was on their break, and The Bear's Claw had quieted.

Marc shrugged. "Not much to tell. I was up there this spring on one of Professor Schulman's field excursions to point out what the weather can do to buildings. There are three up there, two of which are in ruins. The third is standing but not in very good shape."

"What were they?" Gaea asked, taking a drink from her own glass.

"From what the professor told us, it was the original upper campus back in the day. And I mean way back. The one that is kind of intact was Newton Hall. He said the grad students used to live there before the school started expanding toward Orono. It's a mile up that road."

"That is so cool," Gaea said, reaching for a nacho that had just been delivered to their booth. "Ouchy, it's hot she said, taking a bite. Imagine living up in the woods away from the main campus, surrounded by nature. Is there a parking lot?"

"I think so. These buildings were in use until the 1950s. I think most students use bicycles to go to class. Maybe some had cars. There were no abandoned vehicles up there that I could see. The place is actually spooky. I'm not sure I would want to go up there at night."

"I think I saw someone walking up that road near the trees," Himiko said, looking at her friends. "I saw just before coming in here."

"Who is walking up there at night and during a snowstorm?" Marc asked, taking a nacho. "No power is up there, and it is certainly unsafe."

"Look, I'm not making things up here. I really thought I said someone." Himiko emphasized.

"She's not lying," Gaea said. "She did or thought she saw someone. If it were a person, who was it?"

"The Night Witch?" Himiko offered.

"There is only one way to find out," Marc said, eating another nacho. "We go up there."

"In this?" Gaea pointed out the window at the falling snow.

"I'm not ready to hike a mile up into the woods this time of year," Himiko added. "And freeze to death?"

"No, not today. Don't be silly," He said. "Professor Schulman really likes me, maybe too much. Anyway, we have access to snowcats for field research. I think with the right reason, he will allow me to use one."

"Well, it won't be this weekend," Gaea said. "The three of us are going to Bar Harbor to help my sister. And no excuses this time, Himiko."

"I want to go."

"Good."

"That is so cool!" Karen said. The call from Vicky had made her day. "Of course, I will come to help if Mrs. Douglas will let me."

"My mom overrides Mrs. Douglas," Vicky answered. "Besides, I want you here to help with all of this cooking I am going to do, and see my new restaurant. You're really good in the kitchen."

"I can't wait! I'm ready to pack now!"

"It will be this weekend, and you can come up with my mom. She is my next call after I hang up. I know she is coming anyway. This entire thing is my new idea."

"And it's an awesome one! Baking goodies in the new kitchen and selling them at a church bake sale. How cool. The town up there will flip out over your dishes."

"That's the idea," Vicky said. "Let me go and call Mom, OK?"

"You bet. This is going to be great!"

It took all of five minutes of explaining, and Cathy was all in on Vicky's new endeavor. Bill had used it to back out. The last thing he wanted to do was drive up and help clean a restaurant. He would stay behind with Aerin, enjoy a little father-son time, and relax.

His wife, however, was in a mild panic mode. Cathy knew how Vicky was, and if she planned to use the kitchen, the entire building would have to be cleaned from top to bottom, which was no small endeavor. The restaurant had been closed and unused for the last couple of years, so she could only imagine the amount of dust and dirt that had accumulated. A couple of housemaids would not be enough if she wanted to bake this weekend. Cathy called Bob.

"I know exactly what you are talking about, Cathy," Bob said, laughing. "My kitchen here is cleaner than a hospital's OR, and Vicky ensures it stays that way. I also catch her occasionally checking the furniture in other rooms with her finger, and I assume she is looking for dust. She is a neat freak."

"Same with my kitchen when she is here. God help us if someone leaves a glass or dish in the sink. So, I don't think two girls are going to be enough to get that building clean before Saturday."

"I agree," Bob answered. "Let me make a few calls and see if I can get a local cleaning crew in there. I've seen a few advertisements here and there around town. I understand that this bake sale thing is just a test run for her, but then again, I wouldn't put it past her to set up and run full-time, even if it is just the kitchen. She has a very adventurous spirit."

"She is definitely a go-getter." Cathy agreed. "Thank you, Bob. I could make some calls from down here, but I don't know Bar Harbor like you do. I'll be up there Friday night along with Karen, who will assist in the kitchen. This is going to be an adventure for sure."

"We will make it happen. Who knows what will come of this bake sale with Vicky's cooking? I think it just might launch her as a local chef and bring something of pre-notoriety to the…what is she naming the restaurant again?"

"Cinnamon Woodfire," Cathy answered.

"Ah, right. Well, we will see you when you get here. I take it Bill is not coming up?"

"No, he is staying here with Aerin. He is not keen on the cleaning aspect of the whole thing."

"Me neither. Let me get on this."

"Thanks again, Bob."

"You bet."

Gaea, Himiko, and Marc met in his dorm room. He had a computer with a large monitor that he used for his meteorology studies. It was better suited to view the video he had gotten from the UMO Campus Police Department. It had taken two days for his contact to compile the few hours of footage that he had requested. Marc had spent half the night reviewing it until he finally found what might be pertinent to his search. It took him another two hours to clean it up and enhance it.

"We have something," Marc told the girls as they sat down. "I'm just not sure what. I spent nearly all night searching through this and cleaning it up. Let's see why you two think."

The picture started out grainy but slowly became clearer. Gaea and Himiko leaned forward to look at it. Snow was falling, and some flakes stuck to the lens before melting off. Luckily, there were few, as the camera's hood helped protect it from the elements.

The door to The Bear's Claw opened, and a figure appeared dressed in a hooded cloak.

"That's her," Himiko said.

"Are you sure?" Gaea asked.

"I remember that cloak." She replied.

"Look at this," Marc said, pointing at the screen.

The cloaked figure turned, and for a brief moment, a portion of her face was revealed.

"She is Asian!" Himiko exclaimed. 'And she looks like me!"

"Look closer," Marc advised.

Gaea looked closer and saw what he was referring to immediately. "She has a mole to the left of her mouth. Himiko doesn't."

"Great job, detective, " he said, smiling. Now watch. "He resumed the video, and the cloaked girl turned and ran to the left into the night. A few seconds later, Himiko came out through the door and looked around briefly before returning back into the tavern.

"See, not you, Himiko," Marc said, looking up and over his shoulder at her.

"As far as I know, I am the only Asian girl here on campus."

"True. Maybe you have a sister?"

"I am an only child," Himiko replied.

"Maybe she is not a student?" Gaea offered.

"Look where she is running towards," Marc said, rewinding the video.

"There is nothing over there but the woods," Gaea said.

"Yes, there is." Himiko stood up and walked to the window, pointing out. "The road to the old Upper Campus."

CHAPTER 12
The Dead Piano Player

"Really!" Himiko exclaimed as Gaea pulled up to Pepper Mansion. The building's overall size was enough to take one's breath away, and with the snowfall, it was even more spectacular. The scene was not lost on her.

Himiko had never traveled to Mt. Desert Island before and could not stop praising the sights she was seeing. Her arrival at the mansion was the frosting on the cake, and she was in awe.

"You ain't seen nothing yet, Himiko," Marc said as Gaea parked the Jeep.

Staff exited the front door, gathered their bags, and rushed inside.

"Hi, Henry!" Gaea exclaimed, smiling at the butler.

The chauffeur walked up from the garage area and took her keys. As they all entered the mansion, he drove off to park the SUV. Bob and Dottie greeted them in the great room.

"Hi!" Gaea exclaimed, hugging first her grandma and then her grandpa.

"It's so good to see you," Dottie said. "And who is this?"

"This is my new roommate, Himiko Aoki. She is a Junior from California." Gaea explained.

"Welcome," Bob said, smiling broadly. "And it's good to see you again, young man."

"Thank you for having me," Marc replied, shaking the older man's hand.

"Where is my sister?" Gaea asked.

"Where do you think?" Bob said. "At her restaurant, of course, along with your mother and Karen."

"Karen is here. How cool is that?" Gaea exclaimed.

"She came to help with the baking tomorrow," Dottie spoke up. "She is such a lovely girl."

"I can't wait to see her. Gaea stated."

"You will soon," Bob said. "Vicky has invited us all to her restaurant for dinner tonight. It's part of her first trial run before the second trial run tomorrow."

The company Bob Pepper had hired had done a fabulous job cleaning the restaurant, and Vicky had been elated with the results. She was still relying on the old furniture, plates, and cutlery, but it hadn't been long since she had taken over the restaurant. She had already procured accounts with a linen supplier as well as ordered new serveware for the dining room. A technician was coming next month to wire and install the computers that would take orders from servers and organize orders for the kitchen. The system promised to even help control inventory and, with user input, would warn when items were getting low and needed to be reordered. Alcohol would be a major part of the income for the Cinnamon Woodfire. Vicky already planned on hiring a seasoned bar manager, and the new system would make it easier for the person who held the position to perform their duties.

Vicky had made a trip to a local grocery store with the help of Cathy and Karen. Together, they had everything they needed not only for the evening meal she was cooking but for Saturday's bake-off as well. What

Vicky was keeping under wraps was the menu for the night's dinner party at the restaurant. With everything that was being bought, not even Karen or her mother had a clue what the devious chef was up to, and the girl was sneaky and liked to spring surprises upon her guests. She was confident that the evening festivities would be great.

Thankfully, over the last few days, the restaurant has remained quiet, and the resident ghost has not made its presence known. Vicky hopes that on this trip, Gaea might be able to glean some information on who or what it is.

"A Table for five?" Cathy asked, smiling as she greeted Gaea, her boyfriend, Himiko, and the Peppers at the restaurant's front door.

With Karen and Vicky busy in the kitchen, Cathy had taken it upon herself to be the hostess, if for nothing more than to seat the guests. She led them to a table near the fireplace that Karen had lit earlier to enhance the ambiance, and the extra warmth it provided didn't hurt as temperatures in Central Maine had plummeted. The table was one of the larger ones in the dining room and could seat eight patrons and was set for such for the evening. Although Vicky was cooking and Karen would be serving, they would join everyone to eat. Except for the change in courses during the meal. Vicky had been able to get the old sound system working, and the restaurant was filled with the soft sounds of Parisian jazz music.

"This place is amazing," Himiko said, sitting down and looking around at the décor. "Is it going to be a French restaurant? I didn't see a sign outside."

"The sign hasn't been made yet," Cathy answered. "When it opens, it will be called Cinnamon Woodfire."

"Cool name," Himiko replied.

"I love the music," Marc added. "The woman is singing in French."

Placed in front of each chair on the table was a handwritten menu. Bob picked it up and read it aloud.

"A brief culinary trip around Europe. This sounds interesting." He began to read the items listed to himself.

"I love saganaki!" Gaea exclaimed. "And it is not a French dish."

"It's a Greek appetizer," Marc commented, and I love it as well.

"Austrian wiener schnitzel, how yummy!" Dottie said.

"Fettuccini Alfredo!" Bob remarked. "Now we're talking!"

"Look at the desserts," Gaea said. "Vicky is offering a choice of three. Baklava, Palacinke and Apple Strudel. This is going to be amazing."

Karen came out carrying a few bottles of wine, all different and from various countries. Gaea jumped up to greet her and help. Karen kissed her friend's cheek.

"It's so good to see you!" Gaea exclaimed.

"You, too!" She replied. "Grandpa, we are a bit shorthanded here at the moment and certainly do not have a wine steward. Can you open the bottles, please?"

"Of course." He said, taking the bottle opener from Karen.

Karen had found herself calling Bob Pepper grandpa almost from the day she had first met him. She had never known her own grandparents, and after watching Vicky and Gaea, it just came naturally. The older man was kind, gentle, and completely lovable. Bob took to it immediately, and he liked the attention. Every time his "family" grew, he enjoyed it immensely. Karen was a special addition, in his opinion.

"Come help me really quickly?" Karen asked.

"Sure," Gaea answered and followed Karen back to the kitchen.

Vicky was hard at work scrambling between her ovens and two identical 8-burner gas stoves. The wood-burning oven was also lit and had been used to bake the various fresh breads that she was going to serve with supper.

"Hey, sis," Gaea said. "It all smells delicious in here."

Vicky kissed and gave her a brief hug. "Thanks. Now help Karen take all of these plates out to the table. OK?"

"You're the boss."

The entire meal went flawlessly, and everyone had the opportunity to sample every dish that Vicky had prepared. By the time it ended, nearly all of the food had been eaten, and Vicky was elated. Part of the test run was for her to make sure that her portions were correct and not too excessive. The pairing of a few European cuisines was also an experiment that went over well. The combination of French, Greek, German, as well as other countries' flavors had meshed well together. The various wines had helped cleanse the palate between courses. As usual, the German Eiswein was a major hit when it came to the desserts, and pairing it with Italian espresso topped off the experience.

Bob leaned back in his chair and rubbed his tummy. "Bill missed something special. My hat is off to the chef, as usual."

Everyone clapped in agreement. Vicky leaned over and whispered into her sister's ear. Gaea smiled and nodded.

"Take your glasses and these wine bottles. We are going upstairs." Vicky announced.

With Marc's help, Karen quickly put the dishes, cutlery, and most of the pots and pans into the automatic industrial washer. The remainder could be done later.

Karen had turned off the music system as they all sat around the piano bar. Gaea took her seat behind the keyboard, and Cathy beamed with approval.

"What a wonderful idea, Gaea." Her mother said.

"Thank Vicky. It was she who suggested that we all do some sing-along." Gaea responded. "I'm not sure what I can remember and play from memory."

Vicky smiled and handed her a music book. "The former piano player left a few of these."

Gaea took it and read the cover out loud. "Show tunes for the piano. I think this just might work, but I warn you, I play but do not sing very well."

She took a moment to run her fingers up and down the keys of the piano, trying to get the feel of how it played. The converted piano bar was a Steinway, and Gaea knew that the instrument was famous for holding its tone for long periods of time. This one was perfectly in tune.

Gaea opened the book, looked at the first song, and smiled. "Ready? Here goes nothing."

Bob Pepper knew the tune immediately and began to sing in a beautiful baritone voice, to the amazement of everyone sitting at the piano. He belted out *"Hello Dolly"* as if he were premiering on Broadway. By the time the second chorus started, everyone was singing along happily.

Marc's wine glass flew from the piano across the room, shattered against the wall, and everything came to a halt.

"What the…" Vicky exclaimed, standing up.

"I didn't do it, I swear," Marc stated.

"Then who did?" Cathy asked.

Gaea closed her eyes and then opened them. "Let me handle this, " she said, standing up and heading toward the back of the restaurant.

She didn't hesitate and quickly climbed the stairs to the third floor. Upon walking into the room, she called out, "I know you are up here. I saw you run, and the only place you could go was up the stairs. I can sense your presence and will find you, so you might as well show yourself."

Silence.

Gaea closed her eyes and concentrated. After a few seconds, she smiled and walked to the bathroom wall, standing in front of it.

"You are hiding behind this wall." She said, touching it with her hand. "I said I would find you, and I did, so come out and tell me why you are trying to scare everyone."

A man stepped from the wall and into the room facing Gaea.

"How is it possible?" He asked.

Gaea looked at him. He was perhaps in his 60s, with gray hair and pale blue eyes. He wore a suit from the nineteen fifties, and the two-tone wingtip oxfords he was wearing gave away the era.

"Can I see you?" Gaea asked.

"Yes, and also talk to me. Never in many years has anyone been able to do this."

"I can see and talk to the dead. It is a gift I have had since birth." She answered.

"I see, but I'm not so sure I would call it a gift, " the ghost said.

"Why are you trying to scare my sister? She is trying to get this restaurant up and running and make it nice."

"I heard her say she might remove the piano." He said simply. "It was my life when I was alive. It made me angry."

"Why?" Gaea asked.

The ghost turned and vanished.

"Dammit." She said to herself and headed down to her family and friends.

"What happened?" Vicky asked as Gaea returned to the piano. "I was ready to run upstairs."

"Your restaurant is haunted. I'm just not sure by who." She replied. "I do know that it is an older gentleman from the 1950s, and he has an affection for this piano. It seems that he is worried that you are going to remove it."

"I haven't made up my mind yet, but I am leaning toward keeping it. It's nostalgic for the area and I can imagine the thousands of people that sat at it having fun throughout the decades. Hold on a second. I'll be right back."

Vicky ran upstairs and, a few minutes later, came down holding a cardboard box.

"What do we have here?" Bob Pepper asked curiously.

"I found these in a crawl space under the stairs. They are old pictures of the restaurant throughout the years. Most are just unframed pictures, but a few are framed like this one." Vicky pulled out a large portrait that was black and white and framed in a gaudy wooden frame. She placed it on the piano for all to look at.

The picture showed a man leaning against the piano alone. There were no patrons around him, and it was clearly staged as a promotional photograph.

"There are no markings on it," Vicky stated.

"That's him," Gaea said, peering at the image. "That is your resident ghost."

"But who was he?" Dottie asked.

"It might be a guess, but I think he was the pianist at some point," Marc added.

"Good assessment," Bob said. "Are there more pictures in there of him?"

"No. This is the only one." Vicky said, looking through the box.

"He didn't tell me his name, but I am getting the name Douglas," Gaea said, running her fingers over the dusty glass that protected the picture. "Maybe some research can reveal more clues. In the meantime, clean this and hang it on the wall near the piano. Once the man's name, as well as when he was present, is known, and details of his life and death are established, create a plaque to place beneath the portrait.

"Leave that to me." Bob Pepper spoke up. "I have the time that the rest of you don't."

"We also have a lot of baking to do, so let's call it a night," Vicky said, taking the portrait and placing it against the wall on the floor near the piano bar. "I need a new frame for this. This one is way too ugly."

"I'll clean it up in the morning." Karen offered.

Vicky smiled. "Tomorrow is going to be fun."

CHAPTER 13
Upper Campus

Gaea, Marc, and Himiko stayed around on Saturday to help with the cooking for the church bake sale, but were not able to attend the fundraiser. School demanded their attention, and on Sunday morning, the three were on their way back to Orono.

"I still don't get it, Gaea," Marc said. "You say you can see and talk to spirits, and you find this one, and then it simply vanishes. Why?"

Himiko leaned forward from the back seat and touched Marc's arm. "Let me try to answer that. Spirits manifest in different ways for different reasons, and they need energy to do so."

"Like draining batteries and things?" Marc asked.

"Correct." Gaea stated. "Go on, Himiko."

"Well, for Gaea, the ghost does not need to use much energy to be seen, and she can even sense them if they do not try to manifest at all. I think it is one of the reasons that she uses, what do you call it, Gaea?"

"Charismatic shield."

"Some of the dead just are drawn to the living with such a gift. I'm glad I don't have it."

"How do you know all of this?" Gaea asked, looking at Himiko in the rear-view mirror.

"My mother is more than a witch; she is *Itako*. In Japanese, it means a Psychic medium. She can do what you do, Gaea."

"Why didn't you tell me?" Gaea asked.

"I didn't know the extent of your abilities until the dinner party. I think it will help with the Night Witch."

"Yeah." Marc broke in. "What are we going to do about that?"

"Make a trip up to Upper Campus and explore Newton Hall," Gaea answered. It seems that something is happening up there that is related to what's happening at the Bear's Claw.

"What did I get myself into?" Marc said with a laugh. "Witchcraft, ghosts, and the paranormal. I came to UMO to study meteorology."

"What do you think really causes freak storms?" Gaea said, laughing.

"Right," Marc replied. "Let's get back to campus, I'm hungry."

Bill broke down after the nagging from his son, and after a quick call to Clare, he packed Aerin into his truck and stopped by to pick up Logan. The day trip to Bar Harbor would be a long one, and they could stay at Pepper Mansion for the night and return the following morning early enough for the two boys to go to school. Vicky's break-off was enough to drive his son into hysterics as the boy loved his sister's cooking.

The author was still regretting not going up for the weekend and being a part of the meal Vicky had prepared at her new restaurant. His wife had bragged nonstop on the phone for nearly an hour. The problem was that Bill had intended to take his son on some kind of adventure. Writing had intervened, and now the guilt trip was being forced onto him from every direction. The solution was to just go. Sweets could fix everything, especially if Vicky were making them.

"We are leaving now," Bill said. "We should be there in a few hours."

"This is going to be great, Bill. Wait until you see what was baked!" Cathy answered excitedly. "We worked all day and most of the night. I think I gained a few pounds from sampling."

"You better not have." Bill laughed, turning onto the ramp in Wells that led to I-95 north. "If that little bottom grows, I'm not going to like it."

"We are getting older, Bill, so get over it. Your but is not shrinking."

"OK, OK. Fair enough. Be there soon."

"Are you sure, Gaea?" Himiko asked as her roommate returned from the ladies' room.

Marc looked concerned as his girlfriend slid into the booth next to him. The Bear's Claw was somewhat quiet, and a young girl was on stage singing a folk song from the 1960s using an acoustic guitar.

"Yes. She is not anywhere in the Bear's Claw, or I would sense her. Either that or she is very good at hiding." Gaea answered. "She might be able to leave and go elsewhere."

"I thought that spirits were bound to where they died?" Marc questioned.

"If she died on the quad, she would not be bound to a single place," Gaea said as a waiter dropped off the food that they had ordered.

"The dark witch could have banished her," Himiko stated. "I've read that dark witchcraft is that powerful if done by one who is skilled in the rituals and spells."

"Why would a witch want to banish the dead?" Marc asked, taking a bite of his burger.

"The ghost was communicating with Gaea, and maybe the witch became threatened that she would be exposed."

"How would the witch know that Gaea was talking to the ghost?" Marc asked.

"You think it is a girl, Himiko?" Gaea asked her friend.

"Yes. She spoke to me right here at this table before running off."

"I am wondering if she is psychic like your mother."

Both Himiko and Marc looked at Gaea, stunned.

The drive to Bar Harbor took longer than it should have, and it was not because of traffic. Bill had a sudden attack of diarrhea and had to keep stopping to use the restroom. He had finally pulled off at an exit, found a store, and bought Pepto.

He had no clue where the bake sale was, so he went directly to the restaurant, but found it locked, and no one was there. His wife was not answering the phone, so he drove to the Pepper Mansion.

Henry met them in the drive, and a housemaid appeared to take their bags.

"It's just overnight, Henry," Bill said. "Where is my wife?"

"She is in town along with the Peppers and your daughter for the bake sale."

"Perfect. Do you know the address?"

"It's at the First Baptist Church on Pleasant Street, not far from downtown."

"Ugh," Bill muttered. "C'mon, boys, we're heading back to town. Thank you, Henry. See you later."

"Daaad," Aerin complained, climbing back into the pickup truck.

Henry turned, shaking his head, and retreated back into the mansion.

This is all I could get." Marc said, handing the snowshoes to Gaea and Himiko. "The Sno-Cat is in the shop."

"Wonderful," Himiko said, taking a pair of them. We have to hike uphill for nearly a mile, then into that derelict old building."

"My granddad said he used to have to hike uphill to go to school," Marc replied, handing the two girls orange vests.

"Both ways, right?" Gaea said, looking at the vest. "What is this?"

Marc laughed at her offhand remark. "These are safety vests that we use in the field. Wear this, and no one will pay attention to what we are doing. We are going into a restricted area of the campus."

Gaea read the bright yellow writing on it. "Weather Team Research. Cleaver. If people see us, they will think nothing of it."

"What's in the backpack?" Himiko asked.

"It's a standard field pack that we use. First aid kit, flare gun, and other survival stuff. I left the heavy-weather instruments back at the lab. We don't need them. But we do need these." Marc explained, handing the girls a flashlight and a walkie-talkie. "It's supposed to snow again, and I don't want my girlfriend and my new friend getting lost."

"We'd better get a move on before this storm worsens," Gaea said, pulling on the vest. "I would like to go check this out and get back quickly."

"I agree. Let's get going." Himiko said, adjusting her vest.

"I'll lead the way," Marc said, and the trio walked toward the road leading up to Upper Campus.

"What took you so long?" Cathy asked her husband, hugging him.

"Dad got the shits and had to stop a hundred times," Aerin said.

Logan laughed.

"Aerin!" His mother scolded him. "Don't say that!"

"Well, it's true." The boy said and ran off with Logan to find his sister.

Bill shrugged. "You wouldn't believe me if I told you."

"Oh, I think I would." She said, giggling. "Let's go find Vicky."

The bake sale was in full swing, and it seemed that most of the local residents had turned out for it. Vicky was handing out samples of her goodies, and it was working. People were gobbling them up and then buying the cakes, loaves of bread, and pastries she was offering for sale for charity.

Clara Reynolds was not happy with the young girl's new fame and was complaining to everyone who would listen. "I'm the baking queen of Bar Harbor! Not this little harlot!" She said to the minister.

The pastor smiled and took another bite of Vicky's fudge. "Not anymore, it seems."

The woman fumed, turned, and stormed out of the church.

He smiled at Vicky and simply said, "Heavenly."

Snow was falling lightly as the three started their trek up the road that led to Upper Campus.

Neither Gaea nor Himiko had ever worn snowshoes before, but after a few missteps and spills, they were able to use them somewhat efficiently.

"Cross-country skis might have been easier," Gaea said.

"We don't have them in the weather lab," Marc replied. "We had better move it. At this rate, it will be nearly dark by the time we get there."

"And colder," Himiko added.

The snow was deep, light, and fluffy. Marc noted that going uphill with skis would have been impossible. He also could not see any evidence of tracks, humans, or animals on the snow-covered road.

"No tracks," Marc called back to Gaea. "The last snowfall might have covered anything that was here."

An hour and a half later, the trio arrived at Upper Campus. The lone standing building that used to house students stood ominously in the forefront of the dense Maine pine forest. Newton Hall was absent of lights within it as they made their way toward it.

When they entered the foyer of the dilapidated dormitory, it was nearly dark. The wind had picked up, and the three were happy to have some protection from the elements.

"This place is creepy," Gaea exclaimed, turning on her flashlight.

"What did you expect?" Marc asked. "No one has lived here for decades. I'm surprised that some of the windows are still intact."

"Himiko flashed her light down the hallway. "There are the stairs, and look, there are no doors in any of the rooms."

"The doors were probably removed and repurposed for the new campus," Marc said. "Look, I think we should split up and look around the building separately. We don't have much time."

"What is wrong with you?" Gaea cried. "I don't feel a presence, dead or alive, in here, but still, look at the floors. We can get hurt in this house of horrors."

"I'm with Gaea," Himiko said. "We stick together."

"OK, fine. Let's start on the third floor and work our way down. Hopefully, we will find something if there is anything to find. I'm not too keen on going down to the basement."

"Basement?" Gaea asked, alarmed.

"Well, it does have one, I assume. See the radiators?" Marc said, pointing his flashlight at an iron object sitting against the wall. So there has to be a boiler downstairs."

"You go down there. Not me." Gaea stated firmly.

"Let's go upstairs and do a look-through. I want to get this over with." Marc said, heading towards the stairwell.

The third floor was not much different than the first. Every room had been stripped except for an odd mattress and chair that was being claimed by age. The one difference was the common room located at the far end of the hallway.

"Down here! Himiko yelled from down the corridor. "I've found something."

Gaea and Marc hurried toward Himiko from the opposite end of the hallway.

"What is it?" Gaea asked.

"Just look." She answered and pointed to a slightly open door.

Gaea, hesitant but resolute, pushed the door open. The hinges creaked as they stepped inside, revealing a space cluttered with herbs, crystals, and an overwhelming scent of burnt sage. In the center stood an ancient wooden table upon which lay several dusty tomes. The room was large and had an old couch and a couple of chairs that still seemed functional. Marc scanned the walls with his flashlight and could see various faded banners depicting the school's logo, one of the Phi Beta Kappa Society, and other educational societies that he did not recognize. A half-dozen candles sat on the floor near a large fireplace. Marc walked to it and knelt, putting his hand over the ashes within it.

"It looks like it has been used recently, but it's cold now." He concluded.

"What the hell is that?" Gaea asked, shining her light onto the floor.

An encircled star had been drawn onto the wood floor.

"It's a pentagram that is used for witchcraft and to contact the underworld," Himiko answered. "I think we have found the Night Witch's lair. We'd best not touch anything."

"Good advice," Gaea answered, "we don't want whoever is using the room to know we were here."

Himiko nodded.

Marc took out a camera and, after taking a few pictures of the room, put it back into the backpack. "Let's get out of here. We found what we were looking for, " he said.

"Yeah, let's go." Gaea agreed.

They donned their snowshoes and started the trek back down to the quad. The snow was falling harder, the wind picking up, and it appeared to Marc that another significant storm was moving in.

First, the sound of an engine, then the lights came into view down the road.

"Sno-Cat coming," Marc announced.

A few moments later, the vehicle pulled up and stopped next to the trio.

"Oh, boy. Campus Police." Gaea said to Himiko.

"Don't worry," Marc reassured them. "I got this."

The officer opened the door. "You are in a restricted area. What are you doing up here?" He asked.

"Weather Team," Marc replied, handing the officer an envelope.

He opened it and read the paper it held. "This is a Permission form signed by Professor Schulman. It appears to be in order. It's a nasty night to be walking around up here, " he said, handing it back to Marc.

"That's the weather for you," Marc said, smiling. "We're done and heading back to campus."

"Climb in, and I'll give you a lift." The officer offered.

"Thanks," Marc replied, and they climbed into the Sno-Cat and headed down.

CHAPTER 14
Clues & A Mystery

The bake sale had been an overwhelming success both for the church and for Vicky, and her phone started to ring the next day. People were wondering where her goods were for sale. She had to apologize and tell them that she was just setting up shop, and it would be a short time before they would be available, although she would be willing to take individual orders for the time being. So far, she had taken over two dozen consisting of pies, French pastries, and the overwhelming favorite, her chocolate walnut fudge.

Cathy had agreed to let Karen stay for the week to help with the cooking and delivery, but she would have to return to Shaw Manor to resume her duties. Vicky was overjoyed. During that time, Vicky needed to find and hire kitchen help as well as a delivery driver. Bob Pepper once again came to the rescue and offered to set up some interviews for her. He also bought her a new delivery van and promised to have the Chevy painted with the new logo once it was designed. Vicky was ecstatic.

Bob had another issue he was busy with, and that was trying to identify the mystery piano player in the portrait that Vicky had found. If it was a ghost haunting the building, he wanted to know who it was and if it needed to be gotten rid of. So far, the pesky spirit had not caused damage and had not hurt anyone. He felt better that Karen was with Vicky for the week and hoped that she could hire help soon. Bob didn't like that she was at the restaurant by herself for hours on end. Still, the only thing he could do about it was to assist her in hiring help.

Finding a driver proved to be the easiest. Bob sent her a young man with experience in the area and some within-state driving, so he seemed like he would fit in nicely when Vicky was ready to send her goods further than Mt. Desert Island. Vicky had approved of Christopher the moment she interviewed him. His long blonde hair and blue eyes captured her attention immediately. She kept it professional, however.

Finding kitchen staff was proving to be more difficult. Most help was seasonal, and when winter break came, most left the state to work in warmer weather, such as Florida. Four women had responded, and upon Vicky's interviewing, she dismissed all of them. All gave a smug attitude of working for a girl half their age and didn't hide the fact.

Vicky was becoming desperate. She had orders piling up, and now the kitchen staff was. There was no way she could go at it alone.

"Mom, please? It's only for a couple of months until the season starts." She pleaded over the phone.

"She is needed here," Cathy said teasingly. She knew what her daughter wanted, and she had every intention of granting the request. With Shaw Manor, only Herself, Bill, Aerin, a cat, and an elderly dog, Karen, could be spared to help Vicky with her new restaurant and baking business.

"Let me call you back," Cathy said and hung up. Loaning Karen out would not be enough; at least two would be needed. Bob came to the rescue once again and offered to lend his youngest housemaid, Becky, to help.

"Do you want to call and tell her, or should I?" Bob said, laughing. "You are so evil."

"Bill tells me that all the time." She chuckled. I'll call her since I set her up."

"Great. She has been getting orders since the bake sale, and she can't keep up on her own."

"I heard."

"Hopefully, the two will help out enough. I'm still looking for a dishwasher, and I might have found someone. He is on the way over to see Vicky this afternoon. I've never seen a woman so driven."

"Yes, you have," Cathy remarked. "Her name is Dottie Pepper."

Bob hung up the phone and wiped a tear from his eye.

Gaea, Marc, and Himiko were sitting in The Bear's Claw, sipping coffee, talking about what they had discovered inside Newton Hall on Upper Campus. Marc had used an older camera to take pictures and had just gotten the prints back from the local drugstore photo lab. He had decided against using on-campus resources, as going into the building was an offense that could result in expulsion from the University.

"Look at these," Marc said, placing the photographs on the table one at a time.

As Gaea and Himiko looked at them, there was nothing much to see. He had taken shots of various rooms and hallways, and all were devoid of anything of interest. Then Marc produced the pictures he took in the common room. The hand-drawn pentagram and the ashes in the fireplace were obvious. He had also taken pictures of the wall with the intent of capturing the artwork, banners, and graffiti.

"What is that?" Gaea asked, handing the photograph back to Marc.

"I'm not sure?" He said, looking at it closely. "It looks like a chest of some sort. I didn't notice it when we were up there. It was dark."

"It was," Himiko answered, taking it from Marc's hands. She studied it for a moment and handed it back to Gaea. "And I blame myself for not noticing it. Look closer."

"There are markings on it. Oh my gosh. One of them is a pentagram like the one on the floor!"

"I can't make out the other markings. Can you, Marc?" Gaea asked, handing him back the picture.

"No. It's too dark and blurry. The flash must have malfunctioned." He replied.

"I can't make them out either," Himiko added.

"So what is this chest for?" Gaea asked.

"It belongs to the Night Witch," Himiko said. "I have one that I use to keep my spell books, incense, candles, and other witchcraft things."

"How could we not notice it?" Gaea asked.

"It was dark, and it looked like the chest was a dark color as well," Marc answered.

"OK, so what do we do now?" Gaea asked.

"We go back up there," Marc replied.

"It is who?" Vicky asked that night at supper at the Pepper Mansion.

"His name was Douglas Blanchard," Bob replied, handing a folder to her. "According to what is in there, he was a very popular pianist at your restaurant in the late 40s and 50s," Bob answered, scooping a spoonful of his Shepherd's pie. "Unfortunately, he died quite suddenly."

"It says here that he suffered a myocardial infarction and died at the piano! He had a heart attack while playing!" Vicky exclaimed. "No wonder he is attached to the piano bar."

"So wait," Karen interjected. "The restaurant is haunted?"

"It seems so," Vicky replied. "But it's not anything like what we went through at the manor. This ghost is pesky but so far not dangerous."

"It's the so far that worries me," Karen said, taking a sip of her wine.

"We know the right people to handle it if it comes to that," Bob said.

"We do." Vicky agreed.

"What are you going to do about the piano bar?" Dottie asked.

"I'm going to have a chat with my resident poltergeist and hope he listens," Vicky said thoughtfully. "If he behaves, the piano will stay, and I will take care of the instrument. I also plan to hang his portrait on the wall, along with a plaque that tells people his name, the fact that he was a pianist, and the unfortunate event that led to his death. That alone will make a cool piece of memorabilia for the piano bar area of the restaurant. If I find more pictures of Mr. Blanchard, I will frame them and display them. Hopefully, that will appease him."

"That is a very smart idea, Vicky," Bob said, smiling broadly. "If he doesn't cooperate, we rip the damn thing out and have him exorcised."

'I hope it doesn't come to that." Vicky said. "I feel bad for Mr. Blanchard now that I know what happened to him."

"It seems that he was a bit of a sot if you read the police reports in the file," Bob commented. "He had been arrested for being drunk and disorderly a number of times, and it was related to the restaurant and his job. I am thinking that he liked to drink while playing the piano."

"Getting drunk while playing and singing tunes. I wonder why he was never fired?" Karen asked.

"Well, back in those days, the town was smaller, and the community was tight. Everyone knew each other. If he were a local, the police probably would take pity and simply take him home. Getting arrested for drinking and driving didn't happen either. It was nothing like it is today." Bob replied. "Not that I grew up here, mind you."

"It was that way all over the country, honey," Dottie commented, touching her husband's arm.

Bob smiled and leaned over to kiss her cheek.

"Get a room," Vicky said, laughing. "Anyway, Karen and I need to head back to the restaurant to prep for a long day of cooking tomorrow. You up for it?"

"When am I not?"

"Let's get our buts in gear."

"Watch out for the ghost!" Bob called after the two as they left the room.

"Dottie leaned into her husband and whispered into his ear. "Let's go to our room."

"According to Bob, the restaurant is haunted by a dead pianist," Bill said, pouring himself a cup of coffee.

"No way." His wife said, taking a sip of hers. "Are we cursed? Everything our family gets involved in involves spirits."

Bill shrugged. "Supposedly, this one is no threat. I guess it is what we get from your side of the family. Bunch of freaks that can see and talk to dead people."

"What?!"

He laughed. "I'm kidding. Gaea and Aerin are from me as well. You know I have a weird sense of humor."

"You are an ass." She said, stood up, and left the kitchen.

"She went to a new area of the manor that was of her making. A new door off the great room led down a hallway that now had four more guest rooms and two baths. Her destination was the arboretum at the end of the hall. Cathy had always had a passion for plants, and as her career was waning and she was looking toward retirement, she decided to start pursuing her hobby. The glass-domed structure was the perfect solution. It contained exotic plants from all over the world as well as a self-watering system. The spiral staircase that led to the top afforded a splendid view of the plants that were being cultivated, as well as a seating area that looked down at a waterfall that cascaded into a pool that contained aquatic plants as well as Koi and other fish. Botany students from the University of Southern Maine had taken it upon themselves to tend to it as part of their curriculum.

Cathy loved to dabble in the gardens and took delight when something new bloomed or sprouted. Most of the time, she just likes to come and sit, listen to the songs of the water, and let the stress of the day wash away. The arboretum had become her dreamer's hideaway. She looked up and watched as the snow fell and melted on the glass ceiling.

"When do you suggest we go back up?" Gaea asked, watching Marc put the pictures back into an envelope.

"Not tonight. This storm has picked up, and I, for one, is not snowshoeing back up there. I'm not going to be able to get permission from Professor Schulman until I have a valid reason. Hopefully, the Sno-Cat will be fixed. He likes me, so I don't think I will have a problem, but I need to research and find something to go up there for. I'm not sure snow is going to cut it."

"What if I ask permission to go to Newton Hall for an abnormal Psychology study?" Gaea offered.

Marc shook his head. "Not a chance. That building is strictly off-limits. And this time of year, astrology won't work unless it is a very clear night. Even then, why?"

Kimiko nodded. "There would be no reason, and my professor would see right through the lie."

"So it's up to me to figure this out," Marc said. "The only reason to go up there has to be weather-related. I can pass you two off as part of the team. The campus cops are not that savvy as long as I have the credentials."

"It sounds like Professor Shulman really likes you," Himiko said.

"Yeah. I think maybe a bit too much."

Gaea giggled and took a sip of her tea.

She was sure that someone had been there. The protection spell she had cast had been broken, and that much she was sure of. The one thing she was not sure of was who it was. Nothing had been touched or stolen, but the feeling lingered that her space had been invaded, and it was strong. Whoever it was would pay.

A low fire burned in the fireplace. She lit the candles and placed them at the tips of the pentagram. Reaching into the crate against the wall, she pulled a book from its interior. She would have to move the box somewhere else in the hall before it was discovered.

She walked around the pentagram, then stepped inside, kneeling in the center. Opening the book, she began to chant.

CHAPTER 15
Intertwined

The first morning with Karen and Becky was working out splendidly, and Vicky was happy. The baking was progressing nicely, and Becky's addition to helping with prepping and cleaning as they cooked made the process nearly seamless. Vicky could already visualize the kitchen with full staff preparing meals for her customers.

Pots bubbled on the stoves, and all of the ovens were in use, as well as the large wood-fired one. Thanks to the Pepper Mansion grounds crew, the cord of apple wood that Vicky ordered was stacked neatly next to the building just outside the kitchen side door. Vicky was pleased with how easy it was to light and how perfectly it maintained temperature using only the original dampers. The first loaves of bread not only came out perfectly but also filled the entire restaurant with the aroma. The old Le Panyol French-made stove was performing perfectly.

Vicky called a break, as there was time before the ovens would be free. She took a plate of pats of butter from the refrigerator, some of her home-made strawberry jam, and sliced into a loaf of Anadama Bread and offered it to her employees. As they all took a bite of it, they were all smiles.

The bread first appeared in Rockport, Massachusetts, in the mid-1800s. It was somewhat unique in that it included a bit of cornmeal with flour and molasses. Vicky kicked it up with a touch of nutmeg, which sweetened it further. The result was exquisite. It had been a huge hit at the church bake sale and was now in big demand. She had an order for 12 dozen loaves, most from a local restaurant that specializes in breakfast and lunch. She was more than happy to comply.

Vicky had also been busy with other things other than baking, so she was grateful for the two girls' help. Deliveries were starting to arrive that included kitchen essentials such as the cooling racks that she was presently using for the baked goods. Technicians were also coming to check on various things throughout the restaurant, including the installation of her new computer system, as well as repairing the heating lamps over the service counter, and one of her main priorities: having the grand piano serviced and having the pictures of Douglas Blanchard hung on the wall next to it. She had found two more pictures of the pianist in a box under the stairs and had them mounted in a collage. Along with the biography that Bob Pepper had been able to put together, she was extremely happy with the display.

Carpenters had also shown up and were busy renovating the second story to make room for a stage that would host live entertainment other than the piano bar. Vicky was limiting the number of tables in the entertainment area, although food would be served as well as out on the balcony. The bar was being moved and updated, and the large staircase that took up a lot of space was being moved to a more favorable location and redesigned.

Things were moving quickly, and luckily, Dottie Pepper was helping manage a chunk of what was going on. Her mother was coming up to help when she could, but it was a long drive, and she still had her business and Aerin to tend to. Her help was limited.

Luck was on her side that morning when a young woman came into the restaurant with a resume. Denise LaFrance was a recent graduate of the University of Maine, Presque Isle, with a degree in business administration. She was applying for the bar manager's position. After an hour-and-a-half interview, Vicky offered her the position of restaurant manager, which would take a ton of weight off her shoulders. The hiring of staff, as well as numerous other ongoing projects, would be taken over and managed by Denise, including the construction. Once the restaurant opened, she would work closely with Vicky on the day-to-day operations of Cinnamon and Woodfire. Vicky was freed up to run the kitchen. Denise would start work the following day. In the meantime, there was work to do in the kitchen.

Vicky decided to call her dad.

Bill skipped down the grand staircase, whistling happily. He had finished his latest novel and sent it off to his publisher, so he was free for a few weeks until his collaboration with Professor Pickling began. He felt like he was on holiday.

Piddles walked slowly into the kitchen. The boxer's snout was nearly pure white, showing signs of age. Although the dog's eyesight was starting to fail, she still seemed to have her mind and overall health. Apart from a touch of arthritis, Piddles was doing fine at her advanced age.

Bill looked at her and knelt down to pet her and scratched her behind her ears.

"How are you doing, putty tat?" He asked, hugging her.

The dog cocked her head and licked his face.

Cathy walked into the room, interrupting them.

"You never treat Lick that way." She said, walking to the fridge.

"That cat of yours is a Griffin. It hates me. Every time I try to pet it, the damn thing scratches me with its talons. It's evil." Bill said, grinning.

"Lick is not evil!" Cathy exclaimed. "Just a bit shy."

"Shy my ass." Bill went to his wife, hugged her, and kissed her. "Evil-possessed bitch." He whispered into her ear.

"The cat or me?"

Bill smiled again. "I've been trying to figure that out for years."

"Oh, you!" She scolded.

"Vicky called me." He said, changing the subject and sitting down. "She has hired a general manager for the restaurant who is going to oversee things from now on. She will be able to concentrate more on the cooking."

"That is wonderful," Cathy said, joining him. "Last time I was up there, she was having the second story renovated but saving the piano bar. She seemed overworked."

"Just like her mom." Bill teased.

"I have cut back on the work, mister."

"I know you have a babe. And I appreciate it."

Vicky had made the decision to divide the third story to accommodate three small rooms that would serve as offices. One for herself and the other two would be used by the general manager and the bar manager. Construction crews were already busy with the building. The remainder of the space would be her apartment.

Denise LaFrance had taken it upon herself to do more research on the ghost that was haunting the restaurant and found something of interest on the computer that had been set up on the first floor. With construction being done on the second and third, the only viable area was just outside the kitchen and taped off with plastic. Douglas Blanchard had been known to practice witchcraft along with his wife, Melissa. They had one daughter, Mary, who, in turn, had one daughter who was living and attending the University of Maine, Orono. Denise found it fascinating that Douglas Blanchard had married an immigrant from Japan. She copied and pasted the information into a fresh document and then printed it for Vicky. It might be interesting information she might want to use for the piano bar display. Denise shut down the computer and headed outside. The sign company had arrived to hang the wooden carved piece outside the restaurant. Cinnamon and Woodfire were getting their first physical presence.

She also had one of the carpenters measure the faded and torn awnings that adorned the windows on all three stories. Vicky had said she wanted them to be cinnamon colored with light gray trim. As they would have to be custom-made, it would take time, hopefully by the grand opening.

Denise was also starting to put together the restaurant's menu, but it was far from complete. Vicky had half of her dishes chosen, but the bar and wine list had yet to be done. That would wait until they hired a bar manager and a wine steward. Another item on her to-do list was growing by the hour. She was grateful when Christopher drove up in the newly painted delivery van. Once white, it was now beautifully decorated with the restaurant's new logo.

"Great!" she exclaimed, greeting the young man. Boxes are stacking up that need to be delivered—just in time."

"At your service, madam," Christopher said, smiling and bowing.

"Go, go, go!"

As he ran into the restaurant, a man walked up.

"Denise LaFrance?" He asked, extending his hand. "My name is Patrick Durham. I'm here to interview for the bar manager position."

Denise rarely forgot anything, but somehow, this interview had slipped her mind.

"Of course. Take a seat inside, and I'll be right with you after I help load these boxes."

"Let me help." He offered. "I know all too well the challenges of preparing to open and also run a busy restaurant."

She liked this guy already. "Jump in then, and thanks!"

"You bet."

A half-hour later, the two were able to sit down at Denise's makeshift desk to talk. After a few moments of reviewing his resume, she placed it on the desk and looked across at him.

"Impressive, Mr. Durham." She began. "A number of fine restaurants are listed here. Why did you leave the last one in West Palm Beach, Florida?"

"The developer bought the hotel, and it is being torn down. The owner sold it and is retiring and not reopening. Pink slips for everyone."

"I see. And you are also a sommelier?"

"I am. My parents own a vineyard in Napa Valley, so I was brought up on it. It was natural to take the exam, which I passed easily."

"And you have a bachelor's degree in business management from UCLA."

"Yes, I worked in the restaurant business in Los Angeles while I was in high school. After that, I attended UCLA. I've been employed by various businesses since then, usually leaving one job for a better opportunity. I'm not young anymore and would like to find a stable job here. I might consider heading south during winter break, but I am also open to settling here permanently. I am a part-time caretaker for my grandmother, who lives just up the road. Currently, I'm staying with her and I walked to the restaurant today."

Denise wrote a number on a piece of paper and pushed it across the desk. "It is a salaried position, of course. But as the sommelier of the restaurant, you will get a small percentage of every bottle of wine sold at the Cinnamon and Woodfire. And I will expect you to train a couple of the waiters in being basic wine stewards."

Patrick picked up the piece of paper and looked at it. "When do I start?"

"Tomorrow morning early. I understand your grandmother, and we can work around that as needed. Fair?"

"Very fair. And please call me Patrick."

"You can call me Denise. There is no need to be formal here. Let's go meet Vicky, and I'll give you a tour of the restaurant. As you can see, we are under renovation."

"Nothing wrong with that. It will be beautiful come spring."

"Oh, by the way, the restaurant is haunted."

"No way!" Gaea exclaimed.

She, Marc, and Himiko were sitting at The Bear's Claw having breakfast when Vicky called. "I'm emailing you what she found. I thought you might be interested, and it could help me at the restaurant."

Thanks Sis." Gaea said and hung up.

"What was that all about?" Marc asked, biting into a piece of bacon.

"You not going to believe this." Gaea began. "Vicky hired a new manager for her restaurant. She did some digging on their resident ghost, and it turns out he seemed to be a witch."

"No way!" Himiko said. "What else?"

"I'm not sure. She is going to email me shortly with more details."

"So many paranormal things in so short of a time." Marc commented.

"Witchcraft is not necessarily paranormal on its own, Marc," Himiko responded. "The craft is more of a belief and way of life, but some witches and warlocks try to delve into the paranormal for their own gain. It's not a good idea."

Gaea thought for a moment and sipped her coffee. "What if the witch or warlock is a medium?" She muttered.

Himiko sat with her mouth agape at the comment. "That could be dangerous. Very dangerous."

CHAPTER 16
A shocking clue

"I'm going to drive up and see Bob," Bill said, pouring a cup of coffee. "I need to meet with Professor Pickling in Orono anyway, so I thought I could kill a couple of birds with one stone. It would be nice to visit Gaea at the school as well. Want to come? I can take Aerin and Logan, as it's the weekend."

"Logan can't go," Cathy answered. "He is with his parents in Florida. I'm doing a reset of one of the stores, so count me out as well."

"OK. I guess I'll have to call one of my other girlfriends. I'm in such hot demand." Bill said, grinning.

Cathy frowned. "Don't be an ass. I'm not in the mood for your jocularity."

"Ooh, big word." He laughed. "You have nothing to worry about with this old broken-down mule."

Cathy hugged her husband and kissed him. "I wish I could go. Maybe if we finish up early, I can drive up myself and meet you."

"That would be acceptable."

"Acceptable!? I'm calling Bob right now and booking my own room. You are such a jerk."

"Honey!" He said, trying to look at her from under his eyes, and pouting.

She laughed. "Let's go upstairs."

Bob Pepper was pleased with himself, and for good reason. His input and help for Vicky's restaurant gave him a sense of accomplishment that he had not had since he ran Pepper & Pepper Publishing. As a silent investor, he didn't have responsibilities and chose what he wanted to work on with her. The grand opening would be upon them before they knew it, and with the bakery taking off like wildfire, he was a proud grandpa. With Bill and Cathy's adoption of Vicky, she had become a blessing in their lives as well. Not that they didn't love Gaea and Aerin as well, but Vicky was special.

Some might accuse Bob of being old school when it came to his business dealings. He had started driving over to the restaurant to see how things were progressing. Even his wife scolded him for prying. Nothing could be further from the truth. Bob simply loved to watch as Vicky grew in her new role as an entrepreneur. And sampling the goodies she baked was a huge incentive.

He was also impressed by how Vicky was changing the restaurant, making it more attractive and functional for the patrons. He found the new Manager pleasant and well suited for the tasks at hand, and took a liking to Denise LaFrance the moment he met her. The girl was strong-willed, which reminded him of his Dottie. He had little doubt that Denise could help Vicky be successful with the restaurant.

Bob smiled and was interrupted in thought by his phone ringing.

"Bob Pepper." He answered.

"Hey Bob, it's Bill. I just wanted to let you know Aerin and I are leaving soon for your place. Have you heard from Gaea on whether she is coming for the weekend as well?"

"She hasn't called," Bob replied.

"I plan on surprising her at school, as I have to meet with Professor Pickling anyway. Most of the weekend, I just want R&R with you and Dottie and to see how Vicky is coming along with the restaurant."

"Vicky is doing just fine, Bill. What a talented, driven young woman she is."

"Cathy and I are very proud of her. I'm glad you decided to spearhead her project."

"Me too. I was getting a little bored in retirement. At least this gives me something to do."

"I figured that was part of this endeavor," Bill said, laughing.

"Well, Bill. Dottie and I love her like she is our own."

"I know you do," Bill said softly. "She is part of your family as much as she is part of ours."

"Thank you for adopting her and saving her life, Bill."

"No thanks necessary, Bob. Look, let me go. Aerin and I will see you both soon, then we will wing it from there."

"Perfect. Drive safely."

"I can't go this weekend," Marc said apologetically. Professor Schulman is taking the entire class up onto Mt. Washington for a weather field trip."

"In this weather during the winter? Are the roads even open to get up there?" Gaea asked, concerned. Besides, we are starting winter break soon."

The two were at The Bear's Claw on a Friday afternoon, watching a band set up for the evening's entertainment.

Marc was sitting in the booth facing the stage as he watched what he believed to be a member set up a sign near the stage. The man had pale white skin and was wearing purple pants with a bright pink ripped T-shirt. His hair was cut into a mohawk and dyed blue. His ears and nose were pierced, and he sported gold and silver rings. When he stepped away and Marc read the sign, he nearly spat a mouthful of beer all over Gaea.

"What?" Gaea asked.

"Look!" He exclaimed, pointing at the sign.

"Oh my God. What is it?" She asked, giggling.

"Read the sign." He said, wiping the beer that was dripping from his nose.

"Jonny Barfo and the Snotty Dead Assholes? No way."

"They are quite good." A waitress said, overhearing their conversation. "They play retro punk from the 70s, such as the Ramones. Can I get you two another beer?"

Marc looked at the waitress and thought she might be a throwback as well. Her hair was dyed red and piled on top of her head, her nose was pierced, and she wore black makeup, including lip gloss.

"I'll have one more, please," Marc answered. "Gaea?"

She was staring off toward the back of the bar as if studying something. "No thanks. I'll be back in a moment." She stood up and walked quickly toward the ladies' room.

Marc shrugged. "When you gotta go, you gotta go."

Denise LaFrance was busy going through the boxes under the stairs. The restaurant needed some storage space for the new paperwork that was already being generated, so clearing out the old to make way for the new had become a priority. The new storage on the third floor was not ready, and although most of the data that the Cinnamon Woodfire would generate would be digital, a lot would be paper.

Vicky had already gone through most of the boxes, but there were still about half a dozen left to sift through. Denise found what she was uncovering to be quite fascinating. Most of the contents consisted of old papers dating back decades that pertained to the restaurant's operation and could likely be discarded. Two of the boxes belonged to Douglas Blanchard, the pianist from the piano bar. As Denise examined the paperwork, she discovered that he had lived at the restaurant on the third floor until his death.

Most of the papers in the box were sheet music, but at the bottom of the last box was a perfectly bound black book.

Gaea opened the door to the lady's room and looked for what she had caught a glimpse of. Standing at the last sink was a girl dressed in a cloak, her hood pulled over her head. Moving quickly, Gaea walked to the girl, grabbed her arm, and turned her. The hood fell partially back, exposing a startled young blond girl with bright blue eyes.

"I'm sorry, I thought you were someone else," Gaea explained.

"It's OK. Happens all the time. I'm Tracy."

"I'm Gaea. Sorry to bother you." Gaea said, turned, and left.

Returning to the table, she sat down and rubbed her temples.

"What is it?" Marc asked.

"There was a girl in a dark cloak, and I thought I felt something, so I went to look."

"And?"

"It was nothing, just a blonde girl. I guess my feeling was wrong."

"You? Wrong?" Marc chided.

"It happens," Gaea said, grabbing Marc's glass of beer and taking a sip.

Himiko walked into The Bear's Claw, and after a quick hug to Marc and Gaea, she sat down.

"What's up?" She asked happily.

"Weather, boy can't go with us to Bar Harbor," Gaea answered. "He has to go with his nerd friends up to Mt. Washington to measure the depth of the snow."

Marc stuck his tongue out at his girlfriend.

"So, just me and you? That is really cool, Gaea. I'm so excited about this weekend! Vicky's cooking, Yum!"

"Rub it in, Himiko. You think I want to go up there?" Marc said, sighing.

"He does." Gaea teased. "He wants to be the next Marty on the Mountain."

"Who is he?" Himiko asked.

Both Marc and Gaea laughed.

"We need to get going," Gaea said. "I need to still pack a few things, and then we need to hit the road."

"I'm already packed. I just need to grab my bag." Himiko replied, stealing a sip of Marc's beer.

"What's the weather going to be for our drive?" Gaea asked Marc.

"Oh, not good at all. Nor'easter is blowing in soon. Roads will be impassable. Not safe to drive." He said with a grin.

"Jerk." The two girls said together.

As the three prepared to leave, the girl Gaea, who had been confronted, walked by the table and stopped.

"I'm sorry again for the misunderstanding." The girl said.

"No, it was my mistake," Gaea responded. "It was nice to meet you."

The girl smiled, tucked her hood around her head, and left The Bear's Claw. Deep inside the hood, her eyes turned from blue to black. She walked quickly to the road that led to Upper Campus.

The drive to Bar Harbor was uneventful, and the two girls spent the time singing along with the radio and laughing. Gaea decided to stop at the Cinnamon Woodfire to see her sister before heading further out on the island to the Pepper Mansion.

Gaea pulled up and parked next to Vicky's Jeep across the street from the restaurant. The two girls got out of the SUV and walked toward the front door.

"Cool van," Himiko said, commenting on a van that was parked on the street near the restaurant.

"That's one of Vicky's new delivery vans," Gaea replied, opening the door for Himiko. "I think she still only has one driver, so right now, it's more advertisement."

Inside the restaurant, the two were met with a full-on construction site. Crews were busy completing the new stairs leading to the second floor and sealing up the area where the old one once stood. Plastic was taped and hung to prevent dust from permeating the rest of the establishment, which was equally busy installing new electronics. The smell of the baking in the kitchen was a testament to Vicky's hard work.

Gaea led Himiko directly to the source of the delectable aroma.

Vicky was looking over her notes, which she kept on delivery times and what was being sent to whom. She looked up when her sister walked into the kitchen.

"Gaea!" she exclaimed and rushed to hug her. After a long embrace, she greeted Himiko. "It's good to see you again, as well."

"You too, Vicky." She answered with a brief hug.

"Visitors, I see." Denise LaFrance said entering the kitchen carrying a large black book.

"Hey, Denise! This is my sister and her friend Himiko." Vicky exclaimed.

"Vicky has told me all about you and your special ability, Gaea," Denise said, greeting the two.

Gaea smiled.

"I was hoping you could shed some light on this book I found in the storage area under the stairs," Denise said, handing it to Gaea.

Gaea held it for a moment, then closed her eyes, before dropping it to the floor and stumbling back against a kitchen worktable.

"No!"

CHAPTER 17
An Anthropodermic Mystery

Bill decided to make his first stop at the Pepper Mansion as opposed to driving directly to UMO. He had been unable to get ahold of Gaea on her cell phone and could not be sure if she was even on campus. Traffic had been terrible driving north on the Maine Turnpike and it was making not only himself but Aerin cranky. Getting to Mt. Desert Island and regrouping seemed the best option. Aerin was also complaining that he was hungry and wanted Vicky's food refusing to stop at any fast-food place that his father recommended. Bill could hardly disagree. The promise of his daughter's food was irresistible.

"Dad? When are when going to get there?" His son Aerin asked. "This is taking forever."

Bill looked at his son and smiled. "I can't control the traffic, son."

"We could have called Uncle Jeff and gone by boat. It would have been faster than this. He has a helicopter, too, you know."

"Well, Aerin, Uncle Jeff is not available at the moment, so we are bound to do it by car. Unless you want to walk. Feel free."

"Walking would be faster," Aerin answered and turned his attention back to the video game he was playing.

As the traffic cleared, Bill finally reached Agusta and took the exit that led to State Road 3 and eventually that would take them to RT1 and to Mt. Desert Island. He was starting to think that he should buy a helicopter.

"This is super creepy," Himiko said, bending down to look at the book.

"It's more than creepy," Gaea said. "It's pure evil. I've felt something like this before. I'm not sure what it is, but I don't want to touch it."

"It has the pentagram engraved on the cover, but I'm not sure I even want to open it," Himiko added. "I think I know what it contains, but the cover, I mean how it is bound, is really odd. That is not leather, cloth or anything I can think of they make book covers from."

"It is odd," Vicky said, crouching down to examine it. She ran her finger over the surface. "It's a little course, but you're right, Himiko, it doesn't feel like leather."

"Do you want to open it, Himiko?" Gaea asked.

"No. Not yet. I believe it is a book of dark magic, but I want to find out more about it."

"This was under the stairs?" Gaea asked Denise.

"It was in a box with things belonging to Mr. Blanchard the deceased pianist. There were a few more photos, some old newspaper clippings, and this book."

"Can we see the photos and the clippings?" Himiko asked.

"Sure. Let me go get them." Denise said and left the kitchen.

The trip up to Mt. Washington turned out to be a complete disaster. The roads were blocked due to heavy snow, and only emergency snow vehicles were allowed up the mountain. Even the cog railway, which was a reliable way to the summit, was shut down due to inclement weather. Professor Schulman apologized to his class ad nauseam until every member of the weather team was ready to jump off the bus as they drove back to Orono.

When the bus finally arrived back at the weather lab on campus, everyone scrambled to unload and put equipment away—all except for Marc. He decided to head to his dorm room, pack an overnight bag, and drive over to Mt. Desert Island to be with Gaea.

As he climbed into his Camaro, he crossed his fingers. It had been a couple of weeks since he had driven it, as he normally went with Gaea in her Jeep. Camaros were not designed for the heavy snow and abnormal weather that Maine had been experiencing. He turned the ignition key, and it clicked twice before the starter began to turn. Two tries later, the engine roared to life.

Marc sat back and patted the dashboard of the old 1977 Chevy. "Good girl." He said, turning on the heater. Ten minutes later, it was still blowing cold air. Cursing under his breath, he put the car into drive and headed out of the parking lot.

The stop at the Pepper Mansion was quick. After dropping off their overnight bags and greeting Bob and Dottie, Bill promised he and Aerin would be back soon with some goodies from Vicky and left for downtown Bar Harbor.

"Dad, I'm hungry!" Aerin whined. "This is taking way too long."

"We'll be there soon." His father replied. "We could have stopped for a burger."

"I don't want that greasy junk."

"I Don't blame you, Aerin, but it would have tided us over. My tummy is growling as well."

Bill pulled up and was surprised to see Gaea's Jeep parked across the street from the restaurant. He had thought that she was going to remain on campus for the weekend, but he surmised that she had changed her mind. He was extremely happy to have all three of his children under the same roof for a change, although his wife might regret her decision to remain back in Southern Maine when he called her later.

As Bill got out of his truck, he couldn't help but notice the activity in and around the Cinnamon Woodfire. Awnings were being installed above the windows, and he had to pause to admire the hand-carved sign that hung advertising the restaurant. Aerin wasted no time and, taking his father's hand, he dragged him across the street and into the building.

Gaea, Himiko and Vicky had been going through the newspaper clippings and photos for the past hour. They discovered that Mr. Blanchard was involved in a cult that practiced dark magic. He was also rumored to have made a deal with the devil to become a famous pianist. The more they read, the more they realized that the book they found under the stairs was a book of spells that Mr. Blanchard had used to attempt to summon demons.

Gaea felt a shiver run down her spine. She had dealt with demons before, but this was something different. She felt as though something was watching her, and it wasn't a benign presence. She knew they had to get rid of the book, but they didn't know how to do it safely.

Suddenly, they heard a knock on the door. Vicky went to open it and found her father and Aerin standing on the doorstep. She was surprised and delighted to see them there.

"What are you two doing here?"

"It was locked," Bill said and stepped inside to hug her.

"I'm hungry, and Dad won't feed me," Aerin said, joining in a group hug.

"Aerin, that is not true," Bill responded.

"Yeah, right. Greasy burgers and fries from some gross place on the side of the road."

"Yuck," Vicky said, smiling. "I think we can cook something up. How about a pizza?"

"Yummy!" The boy said and charged into the restaurant.

"Gaea and Himiko are here. We were looking over some old things that Denise dug up from under the stairs. Come and see?"

"Sure. I was going to drive over to UMO and surprise your sister, but I guess it will happen here. It's better. Is Marc here?"

"No. Gaea told me he had to go on a weather expedition. How boring."

"Not for him, honey. He's passionate about what he is doing, just like you are about cooking."

"I guess so. We have an issue we are looking at about our resident piano player's ghost. Please take a look. There is a weird book."

"Sure, that sounds interesting, but Aerin and I are both starving."

"Pizza coming up!" Vicky exclaimed. "You can take a look over lunch. Gaea is over there in the clean area. This construction is killing me."

Marc was three-quarters through the drive to Bar Harbor when his Camaro's engine began to make a rapping sound. He quickly pulled over to the shoulder, where it promptly made one last loud clank and quit running.

"Perfect! " He mumbled to himself and tried to start it with no result. Turning the key, he activated the gauges and looked. The battery was fully charged, but the oil gauge was on zero. "Ugh!"

Forty-five minutes later, an AAA tow truck mechanic climbed out from under the Camaro. Stitching on his coveralls over a dirty pocket identified him as Gus. He was an overweight, balding man of nearly fifty years of age. Wiping his hands on an oily rag, he stood up and delivered Marc the bad news.

"The rear main seal on the engine failed, so all the oil poured out. The engine is seized. This car is pretty much junk now." The mechanic explained. "That is, unless you want to have the engine rebuilt or replaced, which will cost more than the car is worth."

"Great, Marc uttered."

"Give me a minute," Gus said and walked back to his truck.

Marc nodded and called Gaea. The call did not go through. "What the?" Marc said aloud.

There was no cellular signal. He was stranded in a dead area.

Marc was clearly frustrated as Gus returned from his truck.

"Does your cell phone work?" He asked the older man.

"Oh, I don't have one of those fancy gadgets. I wouldn't even know how to turn it on. Nope, I have the old CB radio in the truck and it does just fine by me." He answered in a very thick, down Eastern accent. "Where were ya headed?"

"Bar Harbor to meet up with my girlfriend," Marc replied.

Gus grunted and scratched the stubble on his chin. "I'll tell ya what, I radioed into the yard, and they checked the blue book on your vehicle. I'm guessin' it's 1977. Am I right?"

Marc nodded."

"Not the best year for cars and trucks. All of the 1970's car makers produced crap. This Camaro, in running and good condition, is only worth about five hundred bucks. A new engine will cost you maybe triple what it would have cost to have it installed and all. Basically, it's a pile of scrap metal."

Marc cringed.

"Look, son, I think I can help you out. At most, they will pay seventy-five bucks for it. Since you're stuck, I'll give you a hundred and a ride down to Trenton. It's a short cab ride from there into Bar Harbor."

Marc cringed again as the man pronounced "Baa Habaa." He had a feeling he was being taken to the cleaners, but he really had no choice. He had no money to pay for the tow, let alone fix the old Camaro, so he agreed.

An hour later, Gus had dropped off Marc in front of a breakfast café named Wilma's. He shouldered his backpack with the car's license plates sticking out of the top of it. The tow-truck driver honked as he drove away, his beloved Camaro dragging behind. He felt like giving the greasy fat man the bird, but thought twice and entered the restaurant.

Marc sat at the counter and ordered a coffee before checking his phone. There was still no service, and his attempts to make a call proved fruitless.

"Great." He muttered. "Ma'am, do you have a payphone in here? I need to get to Bar Harbor."

The waitress didn't hear Marc and walked into the kitchen.

"Bar Harbor?" A young man seated a few stools down said, wiping his mouth with a napkin and tossing it onto his empty plate.

"Yeah," Marc answered. "My car blew up, so I'm stranded. I'm trying to get to my girlfriend. It was supposed to be a surprise, so she didn't know I was coming. This weekend has completely sucked so far."

"I'm Chris." The young man said and reached out, offering his hand.

"Marc," Marc replied, grasping it.

"I think I can help. I'm heading to downtown Bar Harbor now. Want a lift?"

"You're kidding, right?"

"Not at all. My van is parked outside, and I'm heading back to pick up more deliveries."

"Cool."

"It's the only van out in the parking lot, so you can't miss it. I'll be right out after I use the restroom."

"Perfect," Marc said. He pulled two single-dollar bills from his pocket and laid them next to his empty coffee cup. Picking up his backpack, he walked out the door.

When Chris walked out of the restaurant, he was greeted by Marc, who stood next to his van and stared at it.

"Is everything OK?" Chris asked, walking up to Marc.

"I don't believe this."

"Believe what?"

"You drive for the Cinnamon Woodfire? You deliver for Vicky."

"Yeah. You know her?"

Marc laughed, nodding. "Vicky is my girlfriend's sister. I am heading to see Gaea."

"This is too funny."

"Very fortuitous for me, it seems. You just saved my weekend."

"Well, we best get on the road and get you there," Chris said, smiling.

"Well, it's certainly interesting," Bill said, taking another bite of his pizza. "I've never seen such a book before. The cover is very strange."

"It's certainly not leather, that is for certain," Gaea commented.

It's a book of spells for dark witchcraft. That much I do know." Himiko added.

"It seems that our deceased Piano Player once owned it," Denise commented, turning the book over to look at the back cover. There was no text, just the same strange leathery binding.

Aerin seemed to be uninterested in the book and was happily attacking his fourth piece of pepperoni that Vicky had baked.

"What do you think, Dad?" Vicky asked.

"I have no clue what this is, but I think I know who might."

"Who?" Gaea asked.

Aerin answered before his father could. "Mom, of course."

"He's right. Your mother is a specialist in antiquities." Bill smiled. "Let me try a slice of that Hawaiian. Gotta love ham and pineapple on pizza.

CHAPTER 18
Gatherings

Gaea was overjoyed to see Marc when he arrived at the restaurant. However, she was not so happy about him losing his car. Marc seemed to be letting the recent happenstances slide off his back, so she was willing to let it go as well. If he was happy, so was she. Marc seemed overly grateful for the leftover pizza and refused Vicky's offer to make a fresh one. He and Chris finished off what was left of the four large pizzas that she had made.

Chris dismissed himself to run off to deliver more of Vicky's goodies while Marc looked over the strange book.

"It's weird." He commented. "Himiko, do you think it is similar to what is going on at the campus?"

"Maybe. I don't know a lot about dark witchcraft in the Northeast. I do know it exists and is practiced."

"Maybe this will help," Denise said, placing a newspaper clipping in front of them. "This was in the same box as the book."

The obituary was simple but held hidden clues that Gaea, Himiko, and Marc could relate to. Douglas Blanchard was the piano player at the bar when he died. The cause of death was a myocardial infarction.

"What the heck is a mycando fraction?" Marc asked, squinting to read the faded piece of newsprint."

"Dummy." Gaea laughed. "Sadly, he had a heart attack."

"Oh. I'm a weather guy, not a medical student."

"Wait, check this out," Himiko said, reading further. "He had a wife who died mysteriously. The death was sudden, and no cause was revealed by autopsy."

"What is this clipping?" Gaea said, looking at another snippet from the Bangor News. "It says here that Douglas Blanchard and his wife, Sakura, had a daughter who, after their deaths, was remanded to a local orphan's home. How could Mr. Blanchard have saved this clipping if he were already dead?"

"His wife was Japanese," Himiko said softly.

"Maybe the previous owners saved it. "Marc offered, ignoring her comment.

"But that's terrible!" Vicky exclaimed. "I almost wound up in one of those homes. If it wasn't for Gaea and Mom and Dad, I don't know what would have happened."

"Don't forget our adopted grandparents," Gaea added. "They have been amazing for all of us as well."

"Mr. Pepper makes me feel like I'm part of the family," Marc said.

"So, what is the plan with this book?" Vicky asked. "I would like to know what it is and why it is in my restaurant. Other than, we think Douglas Blanchard owned it."

"We take it to the Pepper Mansion, of course," Gaea answered. "Mom is arriving there this evening."

"If we are going to do that, there is something I want to do first. Maybe you can help me, Gaea?" Himiko asked.

"Help with what exactly?"

"Putting boundaries on the restaurant to prevent the spirit of Douglas from following us to the Peppers. He might be attached to this book."

"Of course. I should have thought of that. Vicky, can we raid your pantry for a few herbs and some salt?"

"Of course you can. Take what you need."

A loud crash followed by a shriek came from the kitchen.

"What the?" Vicky exclaimed, standing up.

"Sorry!" A girl's voice called out. "I dropped the mixing vat."

"That's Kate Oatley. One of the two girls I recently hired as permanent kitchen staff." Vicky said. "Neither she nor Marilyn has much experience, but they are eager and willing to learn."

"It scared the crap out of me. I thought it was our resident poltergeist acting up again." Gaea said, laughing nervously.

"Did you sense his presence?" Marc asked.

Gaea shook her head no.

Chris peeked his head in and addressed the group from the other side of the plastic dust curtain. "All loaded and heading out, Vicky. Will this be the last delivery for the day?"

"It is Chris, and thanks. We're cleaning up and closing early, so enjoy the rest of your evening."

"Oh, your dad is heading out as well. He said he would meet you back at Bob Pepper's, " he said, waving. Then he smiled and disappeared.

Cathy's drive from Cape Neddick to Bar Harbor was pleasant, with no delays. Unlike her husband, she tended to plan her drives when traffic was presumed to be light, unlike Bill, who, whenever he decided it was time, would go regardless of weather, traffic, or whatever else he might encounter.

Such was the case when he decided to suddenly move from Long Island, New York, to Southern Maine during a tropical storm. Cathy could have skinned him alive for being so stupid, although she was happy when he made it to her safely.

As she drove onto Mt. Desert Island, she tapped the steering wheel of her Range Rover, humming to a song on the SUV's radio. Winter was still in full swing, but luckily, the snow Maine had been experiencing had ebbed somewhat, so the roads were clear. Cathy loved Maine in December. Bar Harbor had already decorated parts of the town with festive decorations, including an extremely old and large Douglas fir tree in the quaint town square.

She adored the town and had considered asking Bill if he would consider selling Shaw Manor and relocating, especially during the times when problems were plaguing the family. The move would have been easy for Bill, but not for Cathy, considering her business interests. There were also friends and their son, Aerin, to consider. She did not fancy that her children had to rip up roots and relocate, leaving their social lives behind.

Cathy had toyed with the idea and even kept her eye on the real estate market in the area. Now that she had given management over to Denise Bastien, she had more free time. Gaea was off to school, and Vicky was busy with her new restaurant. Summers seemed open to travel, as Aerin would be out on his break. Cathy Pender was looking at summer homes on Mt. Desert Island.

She knew that stopping at the restaurant would probably be a waste of time, so she passed through town, heading toward the Pepper Mansion. If Vicky was still at the restaurant, they could meet up shortly. Cathy made the left-hand turn onto Old Farm Road that would take her to Sols Cliff Road and, eventually, her destination. She was happy to be back on the island.

Due to her medical condition, she had been an outcast since she was very young. The light was excruciating to endure, so being out during the day when the sun was shining was difficult at best. She had to cover her sensitive skin no matter the temperature and wear dark sunglasses to shade her eyes from the sun's glare. During the winter months, it could be the worst. The sun's reflection off the white snow was blinding to people who were not sensitive to the light.

Medical problems had driven her to get special permission to pursue her academics in an unusual way. Some of her classes were available as evening classes, as they were offered to non-resident students who had full-time jobs and were attending them to further their education. The few not offered in the evening were offered a video of the lecture, and classwork was delivered through a strong box attached to the wall outside of the classroom. Leaving assignments on the professor's desk proved to be unwise, as they were stolen by unscrupulous students.

Her freshman year passed with some difficulty, but as she began the second, the constant harassment and ridicule from students drove her further into seclusion, and the girl's heart began to turn to stone and harbor resentment and hatred for the people around her. Her respite had begun simply enough as she delved into witchcraft, which then led to exploring the darker side. The discovery of a book of the dark arts left to her by her mother and the powers she gained from the spells within it satisfied her when the hexes and curses she conjured worked.

She had also reached out and found others who shared her way of life, and some lived close by. As she learned, her anger and spite grew. The Winter Solstice was soon arriving, and another witch on the campus was becoming too nosy for her own good, which could cost her dearly as the gathering was at hand. The Night Witch lit her candles, crouched down within the pentagram, and began her rituals.

"Are you sure this is going to work?" Marc asked as he watched Gaea and Himiko place a mixture of salt and herbs around the perimeter of the restaurant. Gaea was also sprinkling a mixture of water and vinegar. "How can a salad dressing stop a ghost?"

"All of these are used in witchcraft as well as in the spiritual realm to ward off evil spirits," Himiko explained.

"There are other things as well, Marc, such as holy water and burning sage, but we don't have either of them, so we make do."

"And hope it works." He added. "I don't think Mr. Pepper wants a poltergeist in his home."

"I wasn't considering that either," Gaea said, concerned. She handed the container of salt to Himiko and rubbed her hands together to rid them of the excess. "I hope this works as well."

"I took another precaution." Himiko said joining Marc and Gaea. "It seems that Vicky has a very well-stocked pantry, and there is a cabinet in there that has some very old herbs. I wouldn't be surprised if Douglas were storing some of his things in it that he used for witchcraft and spells."

"What do you mean?" Vicky asked, joining them. "What herbs?"

"In that old cabinet on the back wall, I found herbs and spices that I think were used for witchcraft." Himiko began.

"Oh yeah. The white one that looks like it is original to the building." Vicky said, smiling. "I was planning on going through it and throwing out a lot of the things in it. The herbs and spices in it are old and probably stale. I still don't know why there is sage wrapped in a bundle on the top shelf or what it could be used for in cooking."

"Because it's not for cooking," Himiko answered.

Gaea nodded in agreement. "It's used to ward off evil spirits."

"Correct. And so is the dried Hyssop that I found and used to pack the book in."

"What is that?" Marc asked.

"Hyssop is a powerful purification herb used in magic. It is sprinkled on people and objects to cleanse them. It is also placed in bath sachets and hung up in the home to rid it of evil and any negativity that is hanging around." Himiko answered. "I think it will keep our ghost away from the book. It's kind of like mint." She added.

"It's all very creepy to me," Marc said flatly.

"I was planning on you holding it on the drive back to Grandpa." Gaea giggled.

"The hell I am!" He exclaimed. "Whichever car that thing is going into, I am going in the other!"

"You are such a scaredy cat." Gaea teased. "Himiko will take the book and go with Vicky. You can ride with me if you don't pee on the seat."

"Very funny. I hardly think I'm being over cautious considering the circumstances and what we could be facing."

December in Maine brought an early sunset, and as Gaea and Vicky started their Jeeps, the streetlights flickered on, followed by the Christmas lights that adorned the trees and lampposts that lined the streets of the town. A light snow began to fall, and the flakes flashed as they passed through the lights. On the third floor of the Cinnamon

Woodfire, a dark figure stood in front of the window and watched as they drove away.

Bill arrived at the Pepper Mansion shortly after his wife did, with Aerin in tow. The boy had been remarkably quiet during his time at the restaurant, spending most of it eating pizza and staying in the kitchen with Kate and Denise, seemingly taken by the two young girls. Bill had left him alone and spent his time visiting briefly with his daughters, then exploring the construction that was going on throughout the restaurant, which he had to admit was coming along famously. The restaurant was on track to be ready well before the season began.

Cathy was sitting on a Victorian-era settee that overlooked the great room of the mansion. Dottie was overseeing the decoration of a thirty-foot fir tree that had been erected in the center of the room. The tree towered through the second-floor opening, which was surrounded by a balcony overlooking the grand entryway and the great room below. The tree fell short by ten feet of the glass dome that crowned the space and allowed natural light to flood both the second story and the first.

The tree had to be decorated differently from traditional methods. Because of the height and the limited space, it had been partially decorated from the top down. Placing the large crystal angel at the top of it would have been impossible. Thus, the angel had been placed at the onset of the fir. Dottie had been adamant about using the angel to top the tree, and she had been proven correct. As the sun came through the dome, the rays passed through the glass, creating beautiful prisms of light that danced throughout the room. She had thought that in the evening, the lights that adorned its branches would create a similar effect. That had yet to be seen. The two chandeliers that hung from the second-story ceilings, guiding the way into the two wings of the mansion, would add additional light that should accent the tree and its decorations.

"Dad, I'm going to go upstairs to my room, OK?"

"Sure, just go hug your mother first."

Bill watched his son run to Cathy and hug her before charging off up the grand staircase. The boy was growing, he thought. He walked to his wife and smiled. Standing up, she hugged him and pecked his cheek.

"That's all I get?" He asked slyly.

Cathy frowned and gave him a kiss on his lips.

"It's massive," Bill said, looking toward the tree. "We haven't even bought ours yet."

"That's because we are not buying one," Cathy answered and sat down.

"What do you mean?" He asked, joining her.

"We have been invited to a family Christmas here at the Pepper Mansion, and I agreed."

"Without talking to me first?"

"Oh, please, Bill. You always leave decisions like this up to me. Besides, both Vicky and Gaea are living up here, and Aerin will be off for the holiday break. The staff can look after the pets."

"Fine with me."

Bill was interrupted by Bob entering the room. By the direction he came from, Bill assumed he had been in the library. He watched as Bob walked over and kissed his wife, and after a few words he could not hear, the master of the mansion walked over to Bill and Cathy.

"I'm sorry I didn't greet you both. I was taking care of a few things." Bob said, giving Bill and Cathy a brief hug.

"I thought you retired?" Bill asked with a grin.

Bob smiled. "It seems that I have become the patriarch of our hodgepodge family. Since I am up here and you are down in Maine, I have to take care of a few things as they arise, such as the mystery of this new book."

"Oh yeah, that. I think the kids are bringing it here for Cathy to look at. Are you OK with that, honey?" Bill asked his wife.

"I am excited about it!"

"I am not," Bob said flatly. "From my research, I think the thing is not good at all. I'm not sure how or why exactly, but after what we have all gone through in the past, one thing I believe to be true is that it has something to do with the haunting of the restaurant."

"That would be very unfortunate," Bill said.

"Where are we going to put it?" Cathy asked.

"There is an outbuilding on the property not far from here." Bob began. "It's not in very good shape, but it is intact. We can take it there and examine it."

"What is the building?" Cathy asked.

"The former owner's family crypt," Bob replied stoically.

CHAPTER 19
The Chapel

For the first time that Bill could remember, Vicky didn't seem upset about not being involved in cooking supper. In fact, she was quite happy to have a break from the task and was enjoying herself with the rest of the family. He nudged his wife, and Cathy smiled at the sight of their daughter eating and laughing.

Vicky was indeed enjoying herself, as her workload had been almost too much to overcome. She had more than once second-guessed opening the restaurant's kitchen as a bakery once the renovations began in earnest. Even though she was not Cathy's daughter by birth, she had her drive and determination.

Vicky also had to admit that Lars Andersson, the resident head chef, knew his way around a kitchen. At fifty years of age, the Swedish immigrant had a flair for multiple styles of cooking that made him a perfect fit for a position such as he held at the Pepper Mansion. His style of cooking was not unlike the Fusion style that she had been introduced to during her time in Paris. The ability to combine multiple cuisines into one to create a unique dish was a talent that was nearly impossible to teach. Simply put, it took the culinary arts to an entirely new level. Sadly, the chef was leaving soon for a new opportunity in New York City.

She had found her niche and was content to stay within it. Other than using some influences from other European countries, she loved French cuisine, which she could mix with French Canadian cuisine with an American twist. It seemed the perfect mix to use for the Cinnamon Woodfire. So far, it was working out famously for the bakery.

This evening, however, was all American. The chef had chosen BBQ, and he had done it well. Laid out on the 15-foot-long dining table was a collection of goodies that made one believe that it was the Fourth of July and not the oncoming of Christmas.

Pork back ribs were piled upon one platter and chicken portions on another. Freshly steamed ears of sweet corn filled a colander as well as two tubs of freshly drawn melted butter. Bowls of greens such as string beans, broccoli, and asparagus were available for the family to enjoy. A large bowl of mashed potatoes sat in the center of the table, flanked by two gravy boats. For those who wanted something simpler, hamburgers and hot dogs were made to order. Bob had also requested three cuts of steak that were also cooked to order. T-Bones, Rib Eye, and Porterhouse steaks were available and cut to various thicknesses.

Vicky's contributions included freshly baked loaves of bread and rolls she had brought from the restaurant, an apple, two blueberry pies, and a mango soufflé.

Lars enjoyed it when he could work with Vicky, and any contribution she made to a meal helped him by allowing him more time to prepare other dishes. The girl had a ton of ambition and talent, which made the older man wish he were younger than he was.

"This is delicious!" Bill exclaimed, taking a bite of his porterhouse steak. "Perfectly done."

Cathy had a few baby back ribs on her plate and was happily pulling the bone away from the meat with little effort. The pile of mashed potatoes that she had smothered with pork gravy was making her grin from ear to ear. She nodded her agreement and took an ear of corn.

By the time the evening meal neared an end, the family was having difficulty forcing down dessert, no matter how delicious it was. Once everyone was done eating, most of it was gone, and what was left would be cleaned up by the Pepper Mansion's staff.

Bob sat back in his chair and looked at the people that he considered family and friends, who sat around the table and smiled. How could he not? He had finally accomplished what he had not been able to do as a younger man, and that was to have a family. Granted, none of them were blood relatives, but as he had told his former CEO of Pepper & Pepper Publishing the day he relinquished power, "One does not have to be blood to be family." He truly believed that he had a genuine family that he loved and adored. There were three missing at the table, however. Clare, Bill's literary agent, her husband Doug, as well as their son Logan, could not make it. He would insist on them being at the mansion for Christmas. It had been a long time coming for the old house to be filled with celebration.

Bob leaned over, kissed his wife on the cheek, and squeezed her hand.

"Not at the table," Dottie scolded and winked.

"So, let's discuss this book," Bob said, clearing his throat to get the attention of the room. "It seems that it was found under the stairs of Vicky's restaurant and may have belonged to the resident ghost. I would like to know what is so special about it."

"I think I can answer a portion of that question, Mr. Pepper," Himiko said. "I believe it is a book of witchcraft and a guide to the dark arts. Although I have not opened it, I also believe it holds spells and rituals that would not necessarily be used for good."

"So, it's evil?" Bill asked. "I have had enough of those artifacts."

"Not necessarily, Mr. Pender," Himiko answered. "It is like a textbook and *could* be used for bad intent. It depends on the person who owns it and what he or she does with it."

"I don't understand," Gaea added.

"It could be that Mr. Blanchard came by the book through another family member and if he knew what it was, he became what I call a protector of it."

"I think I get it," Marc said. "I am guessing that it was a family thing, and somehow, Mr. Blanchard came to know of it and what it could do. But who used it originally?"

"We don't know that," Himiko replied.

"Maybe that is why the ghost of Mr. Blanchard is still at the restaurant," Aerin said, taking another bite of blueberry pie.

"Protecting the book." Gaea looked at her brother.

"Where is the book now?" Cathy asked.

"In the back of my Jeep," Vicky said. "Grandpa didn't want it in the house.

"I think removing it from the restaurant may have been a bit premature by the sound of all of this," Dottie added. "But what's done is done."

"Bob, you mentioned an outbuilding where I could examine it?" Cathy asked.

"Yes. It's not far from the mansion. This house is old, and I think older than your Shaw Manor, and it was owned by generations of God-fearing folk. They built a chapel for private worship. The structure has suffered for a time, but it is intact, and relics of the past remain. I think this would be a proper place to examine the book."

"And if the book is possessed like the statue was?" Bill asked.

"I don't think it is," Himiko commented. "But we might have one pissed-off ghost back at the restaurant. I suggest we examine it and then return it to where it was found until we know more."

"Wait," Vicky said, standing up. "Himiko, are you saying that I might be going back to a trashed restaurant?"

"There is that chance, Vicky. It seems that Mr. Blanchard seems to be quite active and physical when he wants to be." Himiko admitted.

"Maybe I should head back to Cinnamon Woodfire." She responded.

"Really, sis? I doubt that you could stop what might be happening, and we can check it in the morning and help straighten things out if needed." Gaea said reassuringly.

"I agree with Gaea," Cathy said and took a drink of her coffee. "I also think that you should be with us to examine the book. You own it after all."

"I what?" Vicky asked.

"It's your building, so you own what's in it," Bob said, a serious inflection in his voice.

"Thanks a lot, Grandpa," Vicky said, sitting down and crossing her arms.

"I think it's time to take a look at this book," Cathy said, standing up and stretching. "Himiko, can you fetch it from Vicky's Jeep?"

"Sure. Vicky, come with me?"

"OK. Let's go have a look." Bob said, tossing his napkin onto his plate.

The winter gathering tended to be a less-than-friendly meeting of witches and warlocks and was more of a tolerance than a celebration. Those who chose to attend did so for their own benefit, not for others of the same ilk. Much could be learned from sharing certain aspects of black magic. This year, it was to be held in Maine.

The letter came in a plain letter-sized manila envelope addressed to the recipient with no return address. No one knew who organized the gathering, nor did they know who sent the letters. Every year prior to the winter solstice, a letter would arrive for those who were members of the unconventional coven and practiced the art of dark magic. The invitation was simplistically handwritten on a piece of old parchment. It listed the date and the meeting place, but no time, as midnight was accepted and had been for decades. Apart from a brief salutation, there was no date on the mailing. This had also been the norm since the witch trials of Salem, Massachusetts, during the later part of the 17th century, as covens had been forced into secrecy and hiding. The document was signed using a red liquid not dissimilar to blood, which was the symbol used by the coven, and had no individual's name or a signature.

Another reason for the winter gathering was to introduce new members who were invited due to a present or past association with the coven, be it a relative or an acquaintance.

The witch folded up the letter and returned it neatly into its envelope. She tossed it onto the dying embers in the fireplace and turned to light the pentagram candles. It was time to try and contact her dead father.

The Chapel was on the far side of the property, but was an easy walk. The Peppers had taken it upon themselves to keep the walkway that led to the building clear and free of overgrowth and debris. Being a Catholic, however, a non-practicing one, Bob had beliefs that were still rooted within him. One of those beliefs was respect for others and their beliefs. The chapel had meant something unique to the family that had built the mansion. Thus, he had chosen to keep it from being taken over by the woods that surrounded it.

Bob, Bill, Cathy, Gaea, and Marc stood at the beginning of the walkway leading to the chapel, waiting patiently for Vicky and Himiko to return with the book. Aerin had chosen to stay behind with Dottie and have a second helping of Vicky's blueberry pie.

"Here they come," Bill said, watching the two girls walk toward him carrying the thick, dark book.

"Why can't we just look at it here?" Cathy asked.

"I don't trust doing that after all that we have been through," Bob said. "I will feel safer in a house of worship."

"I can see that," Bill said. "We have all gone through paranormal things that scared the crap out of us. I was just hoping that it was over with. I do not want anything like that happening here at your home, Bob."

"Neither do I," Bob replied and looked up. "Ah, here they are."

The short half-mile walk to the chapel was pleasant, as the cobblestone walkway was clear of snow and ice, but there was an eerie silence that gave Bill chills. He pulled his collar up further around his neck and chalked it up to it being the dead of winter. If he were a writer of horror stories, this might have been very influential to him. He was content sticking to his genre and writing spy stories.

The trees were devoid of leaves except for conifers such as spruce, pine, fir, cedar, and hemlocks that grew throughout the woods, which allowed one walking the path a partial view of what lay ahead. A steeple came into view, and it was not an especially high piece of architecture, standing only a few feet higher than the surrounding trees. It was painted white but neglected, and the elements were taking their toll as it was peeling.

"There it is," Bob said. "It's in rough shape, but I'm going to fix the old building."

The group walked up to the building and paused to look at it.

From what they could see, the stained-glass windows were intact. Double doors stood as access to the chapel, which allowed a coffin to be brought into the church. A padlock had been added to secure the doors shut. To the east side of the structure, scaffolding had been erected to address repairs to the clapboard siding.

"The job was left unfinished," Bob explained. "Probably due to the death of the patriarch of the family and his wife deciding to sell the estate and move to Florida."

The planks that were once used for workers to stand on were rotted and broken, and the iron of the scaffolding was rusted and eroded.

"It's quite the building," Cathy remarked. "Are you sure you can save it, Bob?"

"Oh, yes," he replied and produced a set of keys. Walking forward, he unlocked the padlock and opened the door, motioning for the others to enter the chapel.

Inside, they were met with an elaborate room. Vibrant tapestries hung from the walls. The artwork depicted various scenes depicting the ages of Christianity, ranging from the crucifixion of Christ to the Last Supper and the Reconquista, the war against the Moors.

As the group walked forward, Bill noticed more details. The chapel seemed more like a church. Two rows of pews, ten in all, led up to an altar crafted from mahogany and inset with marble and gold inlay. A small organ sat on one side of the room.

"A pipe organ?" Bill asked.

Yes," Bob answered, pointing to the pipes that were behind the pulpit.

"What is that?" Cathy asked, pointing to a large ornate marble inlay set on the floor.

"It's the crypt, isn't it?" Marc asked, taking Gaea's arm. "There are dead people down there."

"Gaea?" Cathy asked.

"There is nothing here. Whoever they were passed on a long time ago. I don't sense anything."

"There is a door at the back of the chapel," Bob added. "It is located behind the pipes that lead down into the crypt. I must admit it feels creepy yet calm."

"Can we please just take a look at this book?" Cathy asked. "I would like to get this over with. Why we must do it here confounds me."

Himiko looked at Gaea.

Bob walked to the wall and brought back a folding card table. "Don't ask me," he said, unfolding it and placing it on the floor. The workers probably left it there.

Himiko approached the table and removed the book from the satchel, placing it gently on the table. "I think I know what it contains," she said.

Cathy looked at her daughter. Gaea shook her head.

Leaning forward, Cathy examined the book.

"A Pentagram has been burnt into the cover of the book, not unlike the use of a branding iron on cattle," She began. "And this book is thick, maybe over 300 pages."

'It looks so strange," Gaea said.

Cathy pulled her hand back from the book. "Oh my."

"What is it, honey?" Bill asked.

"It's an anthropodermic bibliopegy."

"What the hell is that?" He asked.

"This book was bound in human skin, which dates it back to possibly the French Revolution. The skin was taken from unclaimed bodies and poor people. I don't think this one was taken from either. Look at these marks that were obviously a tattoo of sorts on the spine at one time. I think it is much older than it appears to be. I'm curious as to what is written inside."

"I'm not sure I want to know," Bill said.

"Hexes, curses, and other dark spells, I believe," Himiko said, looking at Bill. "This is not a nice book."

"Apparently, it is not," Bob added. "I suggest we not open it."

"I agree," Gaea said. "It could be a portal waiting to be opened."

"A portal?" Bill asked.

"Yes, a doorway that allows the dead as well as evil spirits to cross over from their realm into ours," Gaea replied.

Vicky sighed. "So, what do we do with it? I am not keen on bringing it back to the restaurant."

"What about putting it down into the crypt and sealing it shut?" Bill asked.

"How about burning it?" Cathy asked.

"Not a good idea," Himiko commented. "This book is more than just skin and words. A witch or warlock has already put a spell on it."

"What does that mean?" Bob asked.

Himiko shrugged. "Who knows? It depends on the spell or curse. I don't have the expertise to find out."

"What about sending it to a museum that handles things of this sort?" Cathy asked.

The group was interrupted by the door of the chapel opening. Aerin stood alone, dressed in his pajamas. His face was pale, and his eyes looked black. He did not step into the chapel.

"Aerin? What are you doing here?" His father asked.

Aerin caulked his head and spoke solemnly. "She seeks it."

CHAPTER 20
The Grimoire

The witch extinguished the candles and started packing her tools. The Winter Solstice was approaching fast, and she needed to travel to northern Maine. Leaving her belongings behind was not an option; there were people snooping around, and she had discovered that they had violated her sanctuary with their presence. She knew one of them was a witch—though a weak one—but there was another person who could grasp and understand her intentions. It was the medium who concerned her the most. The girl was powerful and possessed abilities that rivaled her own. If given the chance, she could easily read into her thoughts. Being discovered and attracting the attention of the ignorant was not something she could afford.

She stood up and looked briefly into the mirror that hung over the fireplace. Her once blonde hair had turned to ebony, and now it showed traces of white that flowed across her shoulders and down her back. Her eyes, which had once been blue, were now black, and no whites could be seen. Such was the price to be paid to Belphegor, the defiler, a demon she had made her pact with. Selling one's soul to the Devil was the option she had opted for once she chose the life of a Night Witch. She surmised that the more power she had, the easier it was to control those who were weak. She would need to move to her new safe. Her practice needed absolute privacy. Returning to Upper Campus was not an option.

If only she could lay her hands on the Grimoire. The book contained spells and incantations that she coveted. But she had no idea where it was. It was near; that was a given. Her own witchcraft had revealed as much, but it remained hidden from her. A spell or a curse prevented her from seeing its exact location.

The magical book was older than most experts could decipher. She knew it had been in a museum years ago, but had been stolen by a perpetrator who thought it held value. Its monetary value was far less than its magical value. The thief had been caught, but the Grimoire was not in his possession. On questioning, the man refused to disclose the whereabouts of the book or the fact that he had even stolen it. She believed he either sold it or another witch commissioned the thief to obtain it. Either way, it was now missing, and she was determined to find it and possess it. The book held powerful incantations meant for a Night Witch or warlock like herself, and she believed it would greatly increase her abilities. Finding it and obtaining the precious book had consumed her for the last few years. Alas, Belphegor had not given her a clue about its whereabouts, leaving the search up to herself.

She glanced out of a window. The snow was picking up, confirming the weather report of an oncoming storm. The nor'easter would provide ideal cover for her to travel the short distance to the new lair.

Hunger gnawed at her, which annoyed her. Eating was such a waste of time when there were more important things to do and accomplish. Unfortunately, her mortality demanded sustenance. She would need to stop somewhere to grab a bite to eat. Before she left, she tried again to reach out to the Grimoire, and for a moment, she thought she sensed it. Being a psychic medium had its advantages. She tried again, mumbling an incantation and, once again, a faint glimmer, but no more. She cursed under her breath.

Moving swiftly, she dragged her trunk out into the snow and loaded it on a plastic, red children's snow sled. Returning to the room, she gave the space one final look. Finding she had removed all traces of her presence, she shouldered her backpack and left the building. She took hold of the nylon rope attached to the sled and began the long walk to the main campus.

"What do you mean she seeks it? "Cathy demanded.

Gaea walked to her brother, looked into his eyes, and took him by his shoulders. Immediately, they returned to their normal state, and he blinked as if he were waking from a slumber.

"Huh?" He muttered. "What am I doing out here? I was eating a slice of Vicky's pie."

Cathy approached her children. "What's Going on, Gaea?" She asked.

"I'm not sure." She replied. "Something jumped him. Or tried to."

"Jumped him?" Bill asked.

"Yeah, Gaea replied, "Possessed him. It seems to be gone now. How do you feel, Aerin?"

"A little weird. And I'm cold."

"No wonder," Bob said, taking off his coat and wrapping it around the boy. "Running around in winter in your PJs."

"Do you know what jumped into you, Aerin?" Gaea asked.

He shook his head no.

"What's this about someone seeking? Looking for what, "Cathy Asked. The book?

"I don't feel anything happening here or near us. Whoever it was must be somewhere else." Gaea said. "Why, Aerin, I don't know. Maybe whoever jumped him is trying to warn us of something."

"Or is up to no good," Bob added.

"Well, let's decide what to do with this book and get back to the house," Bill suggested.

"What do you suggest, Himiko? You're our expert on the matter." Gaea asked.

"It involves the resident spirit at the restaurant and, I believe, the Night Witch. Against my better judgment, I would return it to the closet in the Cinnamon Woodfire until we can sort all of this out," Himiko replied cautiously. "This book is highly desirable to the right witch or warlock."

"I agree, Himiko," Gaea said. "We can send it to a museum later."

"It's settled then," Bill spoke up. "Let's get back to the house."

The party started to leave the chapel when Gaea suddenly stopped.

"What is it, Honey?" Cathy asked.

"I thought I felt something. Something or someone. She replied, searching for her feelings. After a moment, she said, "Forget it. It was nothing."

Arriving at the mansion, Vicky handed Gaea the keys to her restaurant. "I'm staying here until you get back, and let me know the coast is clear. All of this is giving me the creeps."

"Ok, Himiko and I will handle this," Gaea said. "We will be back as soon as we can. "

"Be careful," Cathy said, reluctantly turning and walking into the mansion with the others.

Bill held back and hugged his daughter. "All of this is something none of us needs. Especially if it is dangerous. I don't want another problem, Gaea."

"Me neither, Dad," Gaea replied, returning the hug.

"I wish we could just get rid of the damn book," Bill said.

Himiko glanced up at the sky. Snow was beginning to fall. "The most dangerous choice might just be to rid ourselves of it. It fell into our possession, so we need to deal with it. Or at least I feel that I do."

"No way," Gaea said firmly. "This involves my sister, and you are my friend. We do this together. We will figure it out and get through it."

"Well, be careful. Both of you." Bill said, turning to leave the girls to their task. "There is a storm moving in, and I want you both back here before it gets bad."

"We will, Dad," Gaea said and turned her attention to Himiko. "Let's take my Jeep."

CHAPTER 21
The Night Witch

Normally, getting to the new location would not be a difficult task. However, the storm would make it just that unless she traveled quickly before it hit. She did not have much time. She would stop in the cafeteria on campus for a quick bite to eat. From what she had gathered, the two girls who were snooping around only ate in the Bear's Claw, so there was no chance of being seen. She wasn't sure, but she had a gut feeling that the two were involved with the Grimoire. How they were involved was a mystery. She was a powerful psychic medium; her skills told her as much. Time would reveal more to her. Time was one thing she was short of.

The trip to the main campus of the University of Maine at Orono proved easier than she had anticipated. The storm was still building, but it moved slowly, much to the relief of the Night Witch. It took only a short time to reach the cafeteria. Fortunately, breakfast was still being served.

Reaching into her coat pocket, she retrieved a still credit card-sized ID. She had received the student credentials when she enrolled as a psychology student at the school. A complete waste of time, she had realized, and dropped out in the middle of her sophomore year. She kept the card, defying the rules to return it to the registrar. The ID still proved invaluable for numerous privileges on campus, such as using the library and eating for free.

Leaving her trunk near the cafeteria's entrance, she walked in and headed to the service area. Most of the students had already eaten, so it was relatively empty, as was most of the food. She chose some of what remained and took a seat near a window that overlooked her trunk. Thievery was practically non-existent at the campus, at least in the outdoors, so she felt somewhat at ease with her precious belongings not being beside her.

She was silently cursing Belphegor when one of the condiment jars caught her attention. The cinnamon shaker was levitating off the table surface.

"What the…" She said quietly.

It hovered there for a moment, then the top started to unscrew, and the shaker fell on its side, spilling its contents.

"Cinnamon." She thought. Then it came to her. She had heard the name before. It was in the Bear's Claw, and one of those girls said it. "Think, damn it. What did it mean?"

It was obviously a clue sent by Belphegor, and she was left to figure it out.

The Night Witch ate quickly, not bothering to taste the school's bland food. Luckily, her new place was close, and she would be able to settle in before conditions got worse. The storm would keep people indoors, and she would be away from prying eyes.

She dumped her tray into a nearby trash bin and returned it. To avoid complications, it was best to follow every school rule. Pulling her hood over her head, she headed back out into the falling snow.

"I am worried sick," Dottie said, placing another dirty dish into the dishwasher. "Bill, why did you let those children go alone?"

"They are hardly children, Dorothy. Besides, there is not much I can do in a situation such as this. The paranormal and witchcraft are out of my league."

"Bill's right," Cathy added. "But I still don't like it. I'm sick of it. Our family is getting caught up in a situation like this."

"It comes with the territory," Bob said, looking out a window at the falling snow. "Having a gifted child such as Gaea. She seems like a magnet for these things."

"We didn't ask for it," Bill said, "And I know she didn't."

Bob scratched his chin. "Well then, we live with her abilities and support her. I love and adore Gaea."

"We love her too," Becky said, and Sara nodded in agreement.

"We all do," Bob said, turning and smiling at the two.

Vicky wandered in from the kitchen, wiping her hands with a hand towel. "I hope those two get home soon. I'm making supper."

"I'm sure they won't be long," Dottie said, taking the towel. "We have a couple of hours left to cook in any case."

"Yeah, I know. I'm worried, too." Vicky said and wandered back to the kitchen.

"Well, I know one thing I can do," Bob said and walked to the phone, picking up the receiver. He pressed a button. "Carl? Bob, here. Can you get a vehicle ready to head into town? Yeah, I know there is a storm upon us. Gaea and her friend are at the restaurant, and I want to be able to go pick them up in case they get stranded."

Bill looked on. He was always amazed at how calm and commanding Bob could be in certain situations. Years of running the publishing house, he surmised.

"Good man," Bob said, finishing the call. "I'll let you know if it's necessary.

The drive to Cinnamon Woodfire was uneventful as the snowfall was still light. Gaea hoped she and Kimiko could return the book to the closet and return to the mansion before it got dangerous to drive. She glanced at her friend as she parked in front of the restaurant.

"Nervous?" Gaea asked.

"Aren't you?" Himiko replied. "I hate having possession of this book." She looked at it lying on her lap. "It reeks of evil."

Gaea frowned. "The sooner we rid ourselves of it, the better. We just need to know how." She turned off the engine and climbed out of the Jeep. Himiko followed.

As they stepped out into the crisp, chilly air, Gaea wrapped her arms around herself, trying to ward off the bite of the wind. The faint glow of the restaurant's lights flickered through the snowy haze, giving a sense of warmth that contrasted with the uneasiness creeping in the pit of her stomach. Even when the Cinnamon Woodfire was closed, it emitted a sense of comfort and hominess, yet both girls felt dread. Himiko shivered slightly, her gaze lingering on the book.

"I can't shake this feeling that it's watching us," she whispered, her voice barely above a murmur. "Like it knows we have it."

Gaea nodded, understanding the weight of her friend's words. "Let's just put it back in the closet and get the heck out of here. We'll find a way to get rid of it or whatever we need to do." She led the way to the front door, unlocking and pushing it open with some effort against the small pile of snow that had accumulated.

The smell of freshly baked bread and cinnamon permeated the restaurant's dining room, lingering from the last time the kitchen was used. Vicky used spice in her cooking and had cinnamon sticks around the restaurant, casting off the scent as a natural air freshener. It added to the ambiance she had surmised.

Gaea led them to the back of the restaurant and into the storeroom. The duo started to make their way toward the closest when Gaea suddenly stopped, halting Himiko with her hand.

"What is it?" Himiko asked.

Gaea closed her eyes, taking in the space around her. Himiko had seen her do it before. She was using her abilities to detect anything out of the ordinary around them.

"Strange," Gaea murmured. "There is nothing here."

"The ghost is gone?"

"More than that," Gaea responded, "I sense nothing."

"I don't understand," Himiko said.

"I sense the residual energy left behind from the living people that were here, but our dead piano player, I sense nothing at all. Not even a lingering hint that was here."

"What does that mean?"

"I'm not sure. It's like Henry was never here." Gaea replied.

Himiko looked around, taking note of the surroundings. "And nothing is out of place. Vicky was worried that Henry would trash the place. Everything is in order."

"A ghost that is not here can do no damage."

"That's true. Let's put the book back in the closet. This is still giving me the creeps."

"Yes, put my book back where it belongs," Henry told Gaea. It doesn't belong to you. It is meant for another."

Gaea looked at Himiko." He's here.

"Who is it meant for, Henry?" Gaea spoke aloud.

Himiko looked around but saw nothing. To her, it seemed as though Gaea was talking to herself.

"That is none of your concern," Henry said, appearing in front of Gaea. "Put what does not belong to you back where it belongs."

"This is my sister's restaurant," Gaea replied. When she bought the building, she purchased whatever was inside it. Including the Grimoire."

"That book cannot be owned, just possessed for a period of time."

"And who determines the span of time?

"You ask too many questions, and I am through with you. I will, however, answer this one last question. The master of the book decides, and he is not of this world. Now, return the book!" The ghost demanded.

"Who is the master?" Gaea demanded.

Henry vanished.

"Let's get this back to the house," Gaea urged. "It's not safe here. I think we should put it in the chapel."

"Why?" Himiko asked.

"Henry is demanding we return it to the closet and that it belongs to some Master not of this world."

"Then it would be dangerous to leave the book here." Himiko surmised.

"I believe it would."

"Then let's get out of here," Himiko said with urgency.

Together, they exited the storeroom and pushed through the door into the restaurant's main area. The storm outside raged in full fury now, fierce gusts of wind rattling the windows like an angry spirit desperate to break through.

They walked out into the storm, and as Gaea locked the door, a Sno-Cat pulled up.

The door opened, and the girls were greeted by a smiling Carl.

"Climb in. The road is too dangerous even for that four-wheel drive Jeep of yours. The snow is coming down in buckets, and even my big pickup can't deal with it. We can come get your Jeep tomorrow."

Gaea nodded and took Himiko's hand, leading her to the Sno-Cat.

Vicky clutched the Grimoire to her chest.

Things had become even more complicated than they already were.

CHAPTER 22
A Difficult Trip

The Night Witch was safe in her lair beneath the campus chapel, which had not been used since the construction of a new building a decade before she arrived. The old building's basement provided the secrecy that was desired, as well as a room that had previously been the residence of the resident priest. It was sparse and small, but it served the Night Witch's purpose.

She discovered the space when she was originally looking for a place to practice her craft. She opted for the upper campus because it was far away from the school and its activities. The further away from prying eyes, the better.

Now that she had been discovered, relocating was imperative, and she could think of no better place. Removing and replacing the old padlock from the basement door had been easy. She had also kept a close eye on the old church and was sure that no one bothered to enter it for any reason, which made it a safe haven.

The basement's lack of windows also allowed her to burn her candles and perform incantations without being discovered.

The lack of a fireplace for warmth was a small nuisance, but the basement proved to be bearable. Wearing proper clothing and having warm bedding would get her through the winter. The cast iron bed that had been the priest's was a boon.

The Grimoire was the most important item she needed to find before the Winter Solstice, as the gathering was approaching quickly. During her descent from the upper campus, she decided to attempt direct contact with Belphegor. The Night Witch had succeeded in doing this once before when she made a deal with the demon to fulfill his wishes in exchange for the powers she sought. One part of the agreement involved the Grimoire and the power contained within its pages. It was time for her to collect what was rightfully hers.

As the storm blew around the chapel, she worked quickly inside, setting up the altar and arranging the items necessary to perform the summoning ritual. Tonight, she hoped she would have answers.

As they climbed into the Sno-Cat, Gaea decided to ask Carl to drive them to the chapel to drop off the Grimoire. She was confident that the Sno-Cat could make the trip easily, even in a heavy snowstorm.

"Carl, we need to go to the chapel before heading home. It's very important that we bring this book there for safe storage," Gaea said.

"This storm is bad. How important is it?" Carl replied, sounding concerned.

"Extremely important. It's a matter of life or death," Gaea insisted.

Vicky nodded in agreement. Carl thought for a moment and looked at the two girls. "I don't know," he said.

Gaea could see the hesitation on Carl's face, and she knew they had to convince him. "Look, Carl, this Grimoire holds secrets that are very bad. It could mean disaster for a lot of people if it falls into the wrong hands."

Vicky added, "We don't have much time. The longer we wait, the more dangerous it becomes. Please, Carl."

He glanced out the window, watching the snow lash against the glass. The storm looked fierce, but the urgency in the girl's voices were hard to ignore. Finally, he sighed, "Alright, let's do it. But we stick together, and if the storm gets worse, we turn back. No wandering off once we get there. In and out, understand?"

Gaea and Vicky exchanged relieved smiles. "Thank you, Carl!" Gaea said, her heart racing with a mix of gratitude and anxiety. She believed that protecting the Grimoire was the right choice. With Carl at the wheel, they had a chance to navigate through the storm and complete this part of their task.

As Carl started the engine, Vicky clutched the Grimoire tightly, feeling its weight in her hands and on her conscience. They were venturing into the unknown, and she hoped that it would be worth the risk. The Sno-Cat lurched forward, and as they pushed through the snow, Gaea couldn't shake the feeling that they were not just racing against the storm but against something much darker that lurked just beyond the veil of the blizzard.

"Where are they?" Marc asked. He was visibly annoyed and paced back and forth in front of the windows facing the drive that led up to the mansion. "They have been gone forever."

"The Sno-Cat is not as fast as a car, Marc," Bob said, smiling.

"I know that. I'm just worried, that's all."

Cathy walked to Marc and hugged him briefly, trying to comfort him. "I'm worried as well, " she said.

"I tried to call Carl, but he is not answering his cell phone," Bob said apologetically.

"You need to put a radio in that Sno-Cat, Bob," Bill said.

"Probably a good idea. It is only used during the winter when it storms, and we normally don't have emergencies such as these. We tend to use common sense and stay indoors during a nor'easter." Bob replied. But, what 's done is done, and going to the restaurant had to be done."

Dottie walked in, and after glancing out the window, she went to Bob. "It looks like the storm has gotten worse."

Indeed, the snow was falling at a rate that was causing whiteouts. The beginning of the drive, let alone the gate a distance from the mansion and the garage, could not be seen. If he had to guess, Marc would have estimated the snow to be some two feet deep, which was enough to paralyze even a town such as Bar Harbor that was used to this type of inclement weather. He was thankful that Gaea was in a Sno-Cat that could handle the snow easily.

Cathy chimed in, "Maybe we should prepare something warm for them to eat when they return. It could help ease your mind."

"Good idea," Dottie agreed, already moving toward the kitchen. "Vicky and I will start a pot of chili. It'll be perfect after they brave this storm."

"Do you really think it will be that long?" Marc frowned, but he felt the tension in his chest begin to ease. "I just wish there was something more we could do."

Carl knew his way around the area, and when they approached the mansion, he veered the Sno-Cat onto a side road that was barely visible through the snow.

"Shortcut." He said simply. "This is an old logging road. It dates back to the 1800s, I reckon."

"Whatever gets us there quickly," Gaea said, trying to see what was ahead of them. For the life of her, she didn't see how Carl knew where he was going.

Carl seemed to sense her apprehension. "Don't worry, I use this road all the time for one thing or another. I know it like the back of my hand. As long as there are no trees down to block our way, I'll get us to the chapel."

As they continued down the winding path, the trees loomed around them like silent sentinels, their branches heavy with snow. Gaea squinted through the windshield, trying to catch glimpses of their surroundings, but all she could see were shadows and white illuminated by the piercing headlights of the Sno-Cat. Carl's confident demeanor reassured her, even though she couldn't completely shake off the unease that came with being off the beaten path. Each bump in the road sent a jolt through the Sno-Cat, but Carl handled the vehicle expertly, navigating the narrow route with an ease that made her believe in his claims.

"Just a little further," he said, glancing at her with a grin that seemed to push away the growing tension in her chest.

"Thank goodness for Carl," Himiko murmured.

Moments later, the Sno-Cat came to a halt.

Gaea strained to see the chapel and could just make it out a few yards away.

"You'll need this," Carl said, handing a key to her. "Doors locked shut with a padlock."

"Yes, I remember." Gaea took the keys and opened the door of the Sno-Cat. "C'mon, Himiko, let's get this over with and get back to the estate." She said, climbing out into the storm.

"You don't have to ask me twice," Himiko answered, following her friend.

The wind whipped around them, blowing stinging snow into their faces. Gaea took Himiko's hand and they waded through the deep snow together. Struggling, the two were able to reach the door.

Gaea unlocked the padlock, and they stepped inside, shutting out the howling wind behind them.

"Hold on a sec," Gaea said and probed the chapel, searching for any sense of a presence. She felt none. "It's ok. There is nothing here."

"Where should we put it?" Himiko asked, shivering. The cold was taking its toll on the Asian girl.

Gaea thought for a moment. "I know, let's put it inside the pulpit up there under the cross. It's either that or we find a way down into the crypt."

"The crypt would not be my first choice. The pulpit sounds good to me."

Gaea and Himiko ran up the aisle leading to the front of the chapel. Stooping down, Himiko could see a shelf within the back of the pulpit.

"The preacher probably kept his bible there." Gaea offered. "Strange, we're putting a book of evil intent in its place.

Himiko nodded and placed the Grimoire on the shelf. "Are you sure we are doing the right thing?"

"It's our only choice for the time being. We can reevaluate once we get back. Let's go."

Himiko nodded, and the two hurried to the exit. Opening the door, they once again braved the elements, headed towards Carl and the Sno-Cat, and climbed into it.

The vehicle rumbled to life, the engine's sounds drowning out the storm's fury. As they maneuvered toward the mansion, Gaea glanced out the window. The snowflakes danced like ghosts in the headlights, swirling together to create a surreal tapestry. She felt a twinge of unease again as the thought of what they had just done crept into her mind.

CHAPTER 23

Theurgy for a Demon

The dimly lit room thickened with anticipation as the Night Witch prepared for the summoning ritual. She had drawn ancient symbols onto the floor that glimmered beneath the flickering candlelight, forming a protective circle that intertwined with the rich aromas of burning incense. She was clad in a flowing robe adorned with intricate sigils, and she meticulously arranged the elements of the ritual on the altar: an iron chalice filled with blood, a dagger, and a small black onyx stone as a conduit, bridging the gap between the astral and physical worlds. This would enable the Night Witch to harness the energy needed to conjure Belphegor. With each of her whispered incantations, echoes of forgotten languages reverberated through the room, tapping into the deep well of dark forces that lay just beyond the mundane realm.

As the final words left the Night Witch's lips, a palpable shift occurred; the room darkened momentarily before a shadowy figure began to materialize within the circle. A flurry of wind danced around them, spiraling violently as the spiritual essence took form, revealing a spectral being cloaked in ethereal light. The Night Witch's heart raced, not from fear, but from the exhilarating rush of connection—finally, she would have the demon in her presence. The air buzzed with energy as the pact between the living and the demon slowly unfolded.

She knew her place and fell to her knees within the dark circle drawn on the floor. The Demon was nothing to fool with and demanded her complete subservience. With what was at stake, The Night Witch was more than eager to comply.

Belphegor stood before her, exuding malice. As a shapeshifter, he had chosen to present himself as a strikingly handsome male human. His muscles rippled beneath his skin, and his hair was as black as coal, contrasting sharply with his vivid red eyes. However, this beauty was deceiving; he embodied pure evil, and she was well aware of it.

"Who has summoned Belphegor the Defiler?" The demon demanded.

The Night Witch lowered her gaze, feeling the weight of Belphegor's presence surrounding her. "It is I, Seraphina, who calls upon you," she declared, revealing her name to him. Her voice was steady despite the tempest of emotions swirling within her. "I seek your guidance and power."

Belphegor's lips curled into a sly grin, revealing gleaming white teeth that only added to his alluring façade. "Your ambition tugs at the strings of this realm, Seraphina. What is it that you truly desire?"

"I seek the Grimoire—the Book of the Dead. It contains powerful spells and incantations that I need to fulfill your bidding. I have been promised the tomb by none other than you, the great Belphegor, and I am willing to make a significant sacrifice in return," she said, lowering her eyes.

"Indeed. Find it yourself." He growled.

"I have tried, my lord, to no avail. It eludes me. There are those who wish to keep it hidden. Those that do not wish to do your bidding."

"You have knowledge of these beings?" The Demon asked.

"I have."

"Why do you not deal with them yourself?" Belphegor spat.

"I cannot, my lord. I am not yet powerful enough for the task. I can accomplish the task with the Grimoire if it pleases you."

Belphegor's red eyes glinted with a mix of amusement and annoyance, his form flickering momentarily like a candle's flame caught in a draft. "You seek power yet lack the will to seize it. However, I will give you the location of what you seek. This is your opportunity, Seraphina. Find and possess the Book of the Dead, for it is yours. For as long as it pleases me. Do not fail me."

"I will not fail you, my lord," Seraphina replied.

Belphegor strode to stand in front of the kneeling girl. Reaching down, he placed his hand upon her head. Searing pain and heat invaded the girl's body, causing her to lose consciousness.

Belphegor laughed, then turning, he vanished, returning to the abyss from whence he came.

It was nearly morning when the Night Witch regained consciousness. She stood weakly, stumbled to her bed, and sat, trying to gather herself. The demon was nowhere to be seen. She rubbed her temples, and slowly, her memory returned along with another very important piece of information. She knew where the Grimoire was. A chapel on the outskirts of Bar Harbor. She used her abilities and concentrated on the book. Finally, it revealed itself to her. In her mind, she could see a restaurant and, within it, a closet. It was there that the Grimoire was being kept or would be kept. She sensed it was on its way to the destination.

Belphegor had lifted the veil, allowing her to see all she needed to retrieve the book. The task seemed too simple; therefore, she knew it wouldn't be. She could also see the powerful medium and the weak witch guarding it. She would have to proceed carefully to avoid being detected by the medium. A spell might shield her from the medium's probing. She hoped.

Another storm was approaching behind the one that was currently dumping snow on the State of Maine, and it was forecast to be stronger. Saraphina would have to move quickly if she wished to accomplish the task and retrieve the book.

Violence might come from her trying to obtain the Grimoire, which she wishes to avoid at all costs. She would slip in, take the book, and retreat into the unseen shadow if careful.

Hurrying, she began to prepare for the drive to Bar Harbor.

The storm had passed, leaving Maine stark white with snow. As it always did, the day after left the air clean and refreshing. It also left a mess for the town of Bar Harbor to clean up. Snowplows had been out as soon as white-out conditions had been lifted, and the seasoned men and women tasked with the clean-up were hard at work. With another storm expected in a couple of days, there was no time to waste.

Marc sat with Gaea at the kitchen table, listening to her tell her tale of the trip into town and the return trip with the stop at the chapel. He wasn't impressed with her and Himiko taking the risk of dropping off the book in a major snowstorm. With another one on the heels of the one that just blew through, he was begging Gaea not to go to the chapel until it was over.

"Gaea, it's just too dangerous. This one is going to be worse." He pleaded.

She looked at her boyfriend. His concern was genuine and compelling, but the Grimoire was immensely important and needed to be dealt with. She had considered shipping it off to a museum. Passing the buck, however, wasn't in her nature. A solution needed to be found to the problem.

"Hopefully, we don't have to," Gaea replied sincerely. Himiko and I need time to figure out what to do with it. It is vastly important to someone; I think that someone is the Night Witch."

"What are we talking about?" Himiko asked, walking into the kitchen and sitting down.

"That book, Himiko," Vicky answered, removing a fresh loaf of bread from the oven and placing it on a cooling rack.

Aerin wandered in and sat down. "Where's Mom and Dad?" he asked.

"Having coffee with the Peppers in the arboretum," Vicky answered. "Want some breakfast?"

"I sure do!" He said excitedly.

"Can you whip up some for us, too? Gaea asked. "I'm famished."

"Sure can. Bacon and eggs with pancakes, ok?"

"Whatever is easy," Marc added.

Vicky busied herself preparing the meal. Gaea turned her attention back to the Grimoire. "So, what to do with it is the question. Any ideas, Himiko? You are our resident witch, after all."

"I've been researching it on the computer, albeit there is nothing about this book. There is some information on books similar to it." She began. "If the book were just a book, we could simply burn it. This is not a simple book, however. It has some kind of spell or curse cast on it, and I don't think it would burn if we tried. We need to break the spell or remove the curse to attempt it. I don't have the power or the knowledge to do it."

"Do we know of anyone who can?" Marc asked.

"Not in this country," Himiko answered. "If we were in Japan, we might be able to find someone."

"And," Gaea added, "we are not in Japan. Next idea?"

"I wish we knew of a cave or something like that to bury it in," Himiko suggested.

Gaea thought momentarily, and then an idea came to her mind. "We have something better right at our fingertips." She said, pointing toward the back of the mansion.

Himiko caulked her head questioningly.

"Yes, Gaea. Enlighten us." Marc said, accepting a plate of steaming food from Vicky. "Thanks."

Vicky smiled and went to load up another.

"The Atlantic Ocean," Gaea said simply. "We sink it to the bottom. The ocean is very deep around the island. A steel box to hold it should do the trick. We weigh it down and toss it overboard from a boat."

Himiko sat with her mouth agape, not even acknowledging Vicky placing a plate in front of her. "That is pure genius, Gaea. And so simple, I don't know why I didn't think of it."

"Why would that work?" Marc asked.

"Two reasons," Himiko offered, "The ocean is the perfect hiding place. The depth alone would be a detriment to anyone looking for it, and the water is a cloak, if you will. It's a natural damper, lessening the magic protecting the Grimoire, essentially negating the spell or curse cast on it, which, in turn, keeps it hidden from prying eyes. It could be years or even decades before it is stumbled upon. By then, the salt water just might have destroyed the book. Its pages are, after all, just paper."

"Where do we get a boat?" Marc asked, biting into a piece of bacon.

"Grandpa, of course," Vicky said, setting the two remaining plates in front of Aerin and Gaea. "Who else?"

"I love the plan," Himiko said, digging into her breakfast. "When do we do it?"

"We need a steel box to begin with. I'm sure Grandpa can help with that as well."

"And we have to wait for the storm to pass and the seas to be calm enough for a boat to go to sea," Marc added. "This nor'easter is going to be rough, and the seas are not going to be safe until it passes."

"That will give us time to obtain the box. That storm is going to be here soon." Gaea said, starting to eat.

Aerin said, "I'm glad I am not involved with all this. I've had enough of ghosts and the paranormal to last the rest of my life."

Gaea smiled. "You are out of this one, brother. Let's finish eating and go find Mom, Dad, and Grandpa. We need to fill them in on the plan."

CHAPTER 24
Even the Best Made Plans

Seraphina's thoughts raced as she processed the implications of Belphegor's revelation. The Grimoire was closer than she had ever imagined, but the presence of a powerful medium guarding it sent a shiver down her spine. She would need to employ all her cunning and wit if she hoped to evade detection. As dawn's last light faded, she began to prepare herself for the journey. She poured over her notes, recalling the spells she had encountered in her studies—defensive wards, cloaking incantations, and distractions. Each one would be crucial in her quest to snatch the Grimoire from its hiding place. She gathered her essentials: a vial of potent herbs for camouflage, the small onyx stone that had facilitated her summoning of Belphegor, and the dagger, which she could use in the case of an encounter.

The Night Witch mentally ran through a checklist of other necessary items that were needed to complete her quest. Her snowshoes were at the top of that list. Trekking through the woods without them would be an impossible task. With everything in order, she left the building and headed for the parking lot where her pickup truck was parked. She hoped that the snowplows had done their job and the roads were clear. She intended to retrieve the Grimoire and return to her lair before the next storm blew in. She would then gather her belongings and head north for the Winter Solstice.

"That is a great idea. "Gaea's father said after hearing the plan to rid them of the book. "Tossing it into the ocean, it should be lost forever."

Bob sat in the arboretum, sipping his tea, listening to Gaea intently. "I can help with the box. That is not a problem. As far as the boat, that can be a little more difficult. There isn't as much sea-faring traffic this time of year as one might imagine. Except for commercial boats. Most of them would be too busy with their work to be sidetracked by what they would deem a useless and time-wasting task. I don't think even cash would sway them. The fishermen I know are set deep in their traditions and how they do their business. I can make a few calls, however."

"There is another possible solution," Dottie said. "The east trail leads up to the cliffs. Bob and I walk that trail in the summer for some exercise. It leads to a sheer cliff that rises some 100 feet from the Atlantic. Unlike most of the island, that particular place is partially sheltered, and I have it from a good source that the water is deep."

"What source?" Bob asked, grinning at his wife.

"The bathymetric map you have hanging in the library." She replied.

"What is a bathymetric map?" Himiko asked.

"It's a map showing the water's depth and other land features under it," Bob answered. "I bought it downtown. I found it interesting and thought it would make a nice addition to the library back when we were decorating the mansion."

"If we need to, we can do that," Gaea said as she poured herself a cup of coffee. "I prefer to take it farther away from land."

"Me too," Himiko replied. "I don't feel comfortable with it being too close to the island."

"I like the plan as well," Cathy said after listening to their conversation. "I especially appreciate that it seems to be fairly safe."

"So, we're in agreement then," Gaea stated, glancing at Himiko, who nodded in agreement. "Let's get everything ready so we can move once the storm clears."

Setting her cup down, Gaea gazed out from the arboretum as snow began to fall once again. She thought about taking a vacation once everything was settled. Florida seemed like a splendid idea, especially during the harsh winter in Maine. After Christmas, she could fly down there for a couple of weeks.

Gaea also wished she knew the location of the Night Witch. Her whereabouts were hidden from her. Perhaps too far away for her to sense. That could be a blessing or a bane. If the witch was able to cloak herself in some manner, she could be close. A dangerous possibility. She felt for certain that the witch was after the Grimoire. A book like the one they guarded would be invaluable to someone such as the Night Witch, and the power she could derive from it was terrifying.

"Gaea," Bob said, standing up, "you can head down to the garage and see Carl. I'm sure he can find a box that suits your needs. In the meantime, I'll make a few calls." With that, Bob left to head to his office.

"Thanks," Gaea said. "Himiko, let's go see Carl. Marc, come with us."

"Sure," He replied.

"Damn," Seraphina exclaimed as she approached her truck, only to find that the driver's side front tire was flat. A delay was the last thing she needed; time was short, and she didn't want to deal with this inconvenience. She opened the passenger side door and loaded her gear onto the seat. Without AAA or a cell phone, she realized she would have to change the tire herself. It wasn't that she couldn't do it; it was the time it would take that frustrated her. She took a deep breath to calm herself.

As Seraphina knelt beside her truck, the cold bit at her fingers, and frustration bubbled beneath the surface. She couldn't afford to waste precious minutes. With steady resolve, she wrestled the spare tire out from the back, her breath fogging in the frigid air. The sound of crunching snow under her boots mingled with the whisper of the wind.

It took a moment to loosen the lug nuts, her fingers struggling against the chill and the rust that had settled in over the season. Each twist felt like an eternity, and the grim thought of the medium tasked with guarding the Grimoire lingered in her mind. She could almost feel the weight of the book pressing down on her, an invisible urgency propelling her forward.

Finally, with a few frantic motions, she replaced the flat tire with the spare and tightened the lug nuts, ensuring it was secure enough for the journey ahead. She packed up her tools with a mix of relief and annoyance. Each minute wasted felt like a countdown to a greater danger.

Once back in the driver's seat, she took a moment to collect her thoughts. While the Grimoire was guarded, she could still approach it if she was cautious and cunning. She would have to use the extent of her abilities to obtain what she desired. Her heart raced at the idea of its power, a wealth of secrets just waiting to be unearthed. But first, she had to get to it, and this mishap had cost nearly an hour.

Starting the old pickup truck's engine, she began the drive to Bar Harbor.

"This should do the trick," Carl said as he placed a heavy iron box on a garage worktable. "It's not too big and not too small. It should fit a book just fine. What did you say you want it for?"

"I didn't say," Gaea replied, testing the box's weight. It was heavy due to its iron construction, and she was certain it would sink like a stone. "We need an old-looking container to store our book in," she lied. "What do you two think?"

"I think it will serve its purpose," Himiko said, also testing the box's weight.

Marc nodded in agreement.

"Thanks, Carl. This will do nicely," Gaea said with a smile at the older man.

"How do you think we should do this?" Himiko asked Gaea. "When is it time to take it to the ocean?"

"Well, we should get the book as soon as possible. We can seal the Grimoire in the box and keep it in the garage until it's time. I would like to have it closer to keep an eye on it, and I will be able to feel if anyone is nearby. I have this feeling that if we wait until the storm is over, it will be too late."

"Too late for?" Himiko asked.

"I believe the Night Witch or someone is already planning on trying to take it, " Gaea answered.

"A gut feeling?" Marc asked.

"Kind of. It's just a feeling that I get when something is going to happen, and when I get that feeling, something usually does."

"We better get moving then." Himiko said, looking out the garage door, "It will be getting dark soon.

Seraphena drove through the town of Trenton and crossed the bridge, arriving on Mt. Desert Island. She had never been to the scenic island and didn't know her way around. She relied on a map she had acquired from the school library. A very important thing it revealed concerned her greatly. The bridge she had just crossed was the only way onto and off the island unless one had a boat. The thought of being trapped by her adversary terrified the Night Witch.

The drive was nerve-wracking, the roads slick and treacherous. She kept her foot light on the gas, mindful of the potential hazards that lurked just beyond her line of sight. Every turn felt like a gamble, but she pressed on. Time was not on her side. As she finally approached the edge of the woods where Belphegor had indicated the Grimoire was hidden, she parked her truck and gathered her gear.

The world was silent except for the soft rustle of snow falling from tree branches. Seraphina took a deep breath, grounding herself, centering her focus for what lay ahead. She whispered a couple of incantations under her breath, feeling the familiar warmth of her magic pooling at her fingertips. Cloaking her presence, she stepped into the woods, treading lightly, aware that she was not alone in her quest. Every shadow seemed to hold secrets, every whisper of wind a warning. She felt a shiver of anticipation—she was close.

Suddenly, a rustling noise caught her attention. Seraphina's heart raced. Had someone spotted her? She pressed her back against a tree, holding her breath. A silhouette emerged from the shadows, and her heartbeat echoed in her ears. The figure was cloaked in darkness, and she felt a chill run down her spine. Was this the medium guarding the Grimoire? "Show yourself!" Seraphina called out, readying her dagger and tightening her grip on her magic. The figure stepped forward, revealing a face she recognized—a face she once knew. A powerful necromancer with glowing eyes and a knowing smirk. His expression held both amusement and challenge.

"Seraphina, I've been expecting you," the necromancer said, his voice smooth like silk yet laced with danger.

"I'm not here for a game," Seraphina replied, trying to mask her fear with bravado.

"Oh, but life is a game, my dear," the necromancer crooned. "And you've just stepped onto the board. You are not so naive as to think that you were the only one in search of the Grimoire?"

With a swift motion, Seraphina unleashed one of her defensive wards, a shimmering barrier spreading out around her.

The necromancer laughed, the sound echoing through the woods, sending an uneasy tingle down Seraphina's spine. "Is that the best you can do?" he taunted. "Let's see what you're really made of."

In that moment, Seraphina understood the stakes. This was no simple mission; her destiny, her very future, collided here in the heart of the woods. The Game was afoot, and the Grimoire's power was at the center of it all. Clenching her fists, she prepared to fight not just for the Grimoire, but for her survival. It was time to use all her cunning and wit, for the night was dark, but it would not swallow her. The end of this chase was just the beginning of something far more significant—something that would change everything she knew. With that thought igniting her resolve, Seraphina stepped forward, ready to confront whatever fate awaited her in the shadows.

CHAPTER 25

The Fate of the Grimoire

Gaea, Himiko, and Marc prepared for the trek to the chapel where the Grimoire was hidden. Gaea appeared especially nervous to Marc, prompting him to inquire, "Gaea, why the urgency?"

"There is someone else searching for the book," she replied, glancing at Himiko. "I believe it's another witch, and a powerful one."

"Do you have any idea who it might be?" Himiko asked.

"I can't tell. They're using some kind of magic to shield themselves. If it's a male," Gaea explained.

Himiko frowned. "That complicates things a lot."

"Complicates things?" Marc asked incredulously. "It makes things a lot more dangerous. I don't like it."

"Is the witch near?" Himiko expressed her discomfort with this new development. The last thing she wanted was to be caught in the middle of a battle between two powerful witches.

"I sensed him last night, but only for a brief moment. I don't think he is close yet, but I could tell he is coming, and there can only be one reason for his arrival."

"The Grimoire," Marc said quietly.

"Yes," Gaea replied.

"We need to get to the chapel and retrieve that book before they do. Things could get ugly," Himiko stated as she examined the iron box. "We may not be able to complete our task."

"We might not have much time," Marc agreed, understanding what Himiko was implying.

"We need a plan B," Marc added.

"Yeah, what do we do with the box if we can't get it to the ocean?" Gaea pondered aloud.

"The winter solstice," Himiko said clearly.

"What did you say?" Marc asked.

"Oh, sorry. I was thinking out loud. It's starting soon, and the gathering is in northern Maine. It's a celebration of witches and warlocks coming together for the Winter Solstice, which marks the longest night of the year. This celebration has been observed since the late Stone Age, when people lived more closely with nature and were more influenced by the changing seasons than we are today. As witches, we meet to exchange knowledge, celebrate, and share information about herbs and incantations to benefit all practitioners. I attended one a couple of years ago, and it was a lot of fun; I learned a great deal. Many powerful witches and warlocks will be present at the festival, and it is not evil. There will be people there who know how to work with the Grimoire," Himiko explained.

"I would prefer to sink the damn thing," Marc said.

"Not so fast, Marc. If—and I do mean if—we can't sink it to the depths of the Atlantic, then the festival sounds like the perfect plan B."

Himiko touched Marc's arm gently. "It is the best plan."

"We still need to get it off the island," Marc said. "Last time I checked, there is only one way off."

"I can cast a spell on the box to help hide it. If I'm not mistaken, that old X-ray apron hanging on the wall contains lead. Lead can shield against many things, and if I was taught correctly, it will protect the book from incantations. But where did that come from?" Himiko asked.

"Carl might know, but we don't have time to ask him. Let's be thankful we have it. It will shield against prying minds as well." Gaea answered.

"We had better get moving," Marc stated. "This storm is coming in soon, and I for one don't want to be stuck in a blizzard."

"Agreed. Let's grab our snowshoes and get a move on." Gaea said.

As they climbed the snow-covered trail, the wind whistled in their ears, foreshadowing what was to come. The air was crisp and cold, and the only sound was the crunch of their snowshoes on the snow. A sense of urgency drove them forward; they needed to reach the chapel before the storm intensified.

As they approached, the chapel became visible, its shape silhouetted against the darkening sky. Tall trees lined the path, their branches swaying in the strong breeze. They exchanged anxious glances, each wondering if the two witches who were seeking the Grimoire were nearby.

"Sense Anything?" Marc asked Gaea.

"Nothing." She answered.

Once they arrived, they pushed open the heavy door, the creaking wood echoing in the stillness. Inside, the chapel was dark except for the dim light that filtered through the windows. They took a moment to catch their breath; the lack of wind in the space contrasted sharply with the howling wind outside. They hurried to the pulpit, and Himiko reached into it.

"It's here," she said, relieved, pulling it from its hiding place. "We must go quickly; those who seek it might sense the book's movement."

"Let's go," Marc said, heading for the door.

The necromancer countered the witch's spell with his own, skillfully dodging her attacks as she moved in and out of the shadows like a nimble cat. He had no time for this nonsense. The distraction was frustrating, but he needed to deal with her before he could locate and obtain the Grimoire. The contents of that book would empower him to fulfill his destiny as a necromancer: to revive the dead and enslave them. He was not about to bow to the whims of a weak young witch.

"Give it up! The Grimoire is mine!" the necromancer called out. But he was met with silence. He listened intently for her, but the only sound was of the wind.

He could not have dispatched of her that easily, could he? Carefully, he stepped into the open and searched for her.

Seraphina knew she could not defeat the necromancer. He was simply too powerful. He only chance was to trick him and slip away. If she could reach the book before him, she believed she could evade detection and make her escape.

She had mastered a powerful spell that was highly useful for avoiding detection, allowing her to navigate the University of Maine campus discreetly. Belphegor had given her the incantation as part of their pact, and now it seemed invaluable in her current predicament.

First, Seraphina cast a spell to distract the necromancer. Then, she prepared a pyrotechnic spell that would create a bright flash of light, but it would be delayed by a few moments. Finally, she cast her avoidance spell and made her escape toward the Grimoire.

In the open air, the necromancer realized he had made a tactical error when a bright flash of light temporarily blinded him in the darkness of the night. The flash lasted only a few moments, but it left him grasping a tree as he tried to regain his vision. "What the hell?" he thought.

By the time the necromancer regained his sight, Seraphina was approaching her destination, which she hoped would lead her to the Grimoire.

The necromancer searched the area for some time but found no sign of the witch. He had been duped. He had let her get ahead of him, and with the storm worsening with every moment, it was going to prove difficult to catch her before she had the book.

If he did catch her, he thought he just might dispose of her. On a second consideration, getting rid of the body would be too troublesome. He would render her unconscious and make away with the Grimoire.

"Damn it to hell." He swore under his breath and took off after her.

The trick had worked well so far. The Night Witch was far ahead of the necromancer and believed she would find the book with enough time to escape. The storm was intensifying, and although it would slow her down, it would also help keep her hidden. She knew the Grimoire was near; she could feel it calling her.

Seraphina was hoping to find the Grimoire quickly. However, the search was proving to be difficult at best. The small space was dark and relatively cluttered, and the book could be hidden anywhere. To make things worse, chapels such as the one she was in were old, and there was usually a crypt beneath them. The last thing she wanted to do was to crawl around a dark room filled with dead bodies.

She hoped she would not be discovered by the medium or the necromancer. Reaching into her backpack, she retrieved a flashlight. Using it to search was risky, but necessary.

Thirty minutes later, she had become enraged. The Grimoire was not in the chapel, and she didn't think it was in the crypt. She couldn't sense the book anymore as she had when she was on campus. Had Belphegor misled her. She dismissed the thought. He wanted her to obtain the book more than she desired it. It had been taken from the chapel by the medium or the necromancer, who had gotten here before she did. If so, she had failed.

"Think." She spoke to herself. "Where could it be?"

Her train of thought was broken by the necromancer entering the chapel. She looked at him and sat on one of the chapel pews.

"Forget it. It's gone." She said softly.

"Gone? How is that possible?" The necromancer demanded. "By whom?"

"At first, I thought you had gotten her before me." She answered and thought for a moment. "It was the medium and the weak witch."

"Tell me of this medium and witch?"

Gaea, Himiko, and Marc finished wrapping the Grimoire in a lead apron and sealing it inside an iron box just as Seraphina cast her pyrotechnic spell at the necromancer.

"That does it," Himiko said. "Now, where should we hide it?"

"What's wrong, Gaea?" Marc asked, noticing his girlfriend's troubled expression.

"There are two of them. They're in the chapel," she replied. "They know the book has been taken."

"Do they know where we are?" Himiko asked.

"I don't think so. To them, we're just people in the crowd. They can't differentiate; the witch is too weak of a medium."

"What about the Grimoire?" Marc asked, hanging up his and the girls' snowshoes.

"They can't sense it," Gaea replied. The lead, the box, and Himiko's spell are hiding it from them. I can tell, but I don't know how I can. I just can."

"So, we are safe?" Marc asked.

"I think we're safe as long as we stay here," Gaea suggested. "They will be searching for someone trying to leave the island. They have no idea that we have a safe haven in the mansion. The Night Witch probably assumes we're heading for the university. When we do go, we won't have the Grimoire with us."

"Where do we hide the box?" Himiko asked.

"Let's put it down in the old root cellar in the garage," Gaea replied.

"Good thinking. The depth and the earth itself will help shield it," Himiko agreed.

Marc picked up the box and followed Gaea to the door set in the concrete floor near the rear of the garage.

"Turn on that switch," Gaea instructed as she opened the door. The damp smell of earth assaulted their nostrils.

Himiko flipped the switch, and the three of them walked down a wooden flight of stairs.

Seraphina provided him with a brief account of the two girls who had gotten hold of the Grimoire. "So, they have the book, or at least I believe they do," she concluded.

"And where are they? You are the medium, Seraphina," he demanded.

"I don't know," she hissed back at him. "I don't sense them or the Grimoire. They have vanished."

"You never had a very strong gift. Your mother knew this when you were a baby," he said, sitting down next to her.

"Father, that book is promised to me," she asserted.

"By whom?" he asked.

"I made a pact," she replied.

"A pact with whom or what?" he inquired.

"Belphegor, the defiler," she said, looking him in the eye.

"Foolish girl. Now we have to retrieve that book, or the demon will destroy you," he warned. Your soul may yet be saved.

She nodded and sighed. "But how?"

"We wait. We wait for them to make a mistake, then we will take the Grimoire, uncover its secrets, and return it to its rightful owner."

"You will help me?"

"You are my daughter, and I, too, desire the Grimoire intensely. I believe it will take both of us to retrieve it."

"What will we do until then?" She asked.

"We travel to the gathering together. Perhaps the medium and the witch will go there with the Grimoire. The chance of them doing so is remote, yet people tend to do stupid things. If they do, we will confront them and take the book."

"Very well. I will go with you."

CHAPTER 26
A Grim Pepper Christmas

Two weeks had passed, and Gaea sensed no trace of either individual who had attempted to take the Grimoire. This brought some relief to the Pepper and Pender families and the mansion's staff.

Preparations for the Christmas celebrations were in full swing, all under the watchful eye of Dottie Pepper, who had a keen eye for detail, right down to the last piece of tinsel placed on the tree.

Aerin continuously pestered Gaea, Marc, and Himiko for details about retrieving the book, but he was met with silence. The three would not share any information about the Grimoire's location, only stating that it was "in a safe place." This vague response frustrated Aerin immensely. Gaea knew he would likely search the estate grounds for it, but she was confident he would find nothing, despite being a powerful medium. The precautions in place were designed to thwart even his attempts, even though the book was much closer than he realized.

Bill and Bob were spending most of their time in Bob's library whenever Bill wasn't writing. Bob had set up an office for Bill to encourage more visits from the novelist and his family. So far, this strategy was paying off. The harsh winter weather had helped keep the Penders at the mansion for an extended visit. The situation with Gaea and Himiko regarding the Grimoire had also kept them nearby. With Christmas approaching, Bob Pepper could not be happier.

Cathy was busy assisting Dottie, while Vicky spent most of her time in the kitchen at the estate or Cinnamon Woodfire, as the weather had improved since the last nor'easter.

Luckily, the next storm wasn't due until Christmas, two days away, giving time for last-minute shopping for those who had not completed their lists. Bill was the only guilty party and was made apparent when he announced an impromptu trip into town. No one believed his lame excuse of going in to help Vicky at the restaurant. It was her husband's modus operandi, Cathy explained.

On this day, Vicky was at the mansion preparing for Christmas dinner since the restaurant was closed for the holiday. She had given her staff a paid week off along with a generous Christmas bonus. She had planned on an apple cider-glazed ham with traditional Maine sides such as clam chowder and fresh assorted vegetables. Of course, there would be two or three freshly baked desserts along with homemade ice cream from a local dairy farm. With the staff and Dottie's help, she fully anticipated a delicious holiday meal.

As the day unfolded, the once delightful aromas of spices and herbs twisted strange and unnerving scents through the mansion, beckoning everyone into the kitchen. Vicky, practical yet stylish with her hair pulled back in a taut bun, moved with a tense urgency, her voice issuing hurried commands to Dottie and Cathy, who were chopping vegetables with an intensity that seemed almost frenetic.

"Can you feel it?" Cathy murmured, her eyes darting nervously around the room as she set napkins beside each plate, her movements jittery. "Christmas is closer than ever."

"It feels... different this year," Dottie whispered, her warm gaze replaced with a chill, as shadows flickered in the corners of the room. "With everyone here, it feels almost like a gathering of... spirits."

In the cozy corner of the living room, Marc and Himiko engaged in a hushed yet tense conversation, their expressions strained as they exchanged worried glances regarding their upcoming trip to the Winter Solstice Festival.

"What if they are there?" Marc whispered, his brow knitted with anxiety. "That book should never be meddled with."

Himiko nodded, her voice hushed, "I don't think they will be at the festival we are attending, but I have heard of another gathering. And it's not so friendly."

"Another festival?" Marc asked.

Suddenly, Gaea appeared in the doorway, her hands shoved deep into the pockets of her kitchen apron. Her expression was a mix of curiosity and caution. "What are you two whispering about?" she asked, narrowing her eyes with suspicion. "You're supposed to be helping."

"It's about the festival," Marc admitted. "Himiko was telling me about another gathering that the two individuals who are after the book might be attending."

"Oh?" Gaea replied, intrigued.

"I'm afraid it might be real," Himiko began. "I've only heard of it from a reliable source. As the saying goes, good cannot exist without evil. The Winter Solstice Festival celebrates life and the arrival of a new year of prosperity, while another gathering, which remains unnamed and shrouded in secrecy, celebrates death and dark magic. I've heard it's invitation-only."

"And you think the Night Witch will attend it?" Gaea asked.

"It would make sense, wouldn't it?" Himiko said, pulling the curtain aside to glance out the window. Snow was falling once again.

Marc looked visibly anxious as he fidgeted with his feet. "We will have to bring this up with your parents and the Peppers."

"I know, and I'm not looking forward to it. They think this entire ordeal is over with." Gaea stepped closer to the window, watching as the snowflakes danced down, each unique against the pristine white blanket slowly covering the ground. "It's not just the weather, is it? It's everything happening around us."

Himiko furrowed her brow. "Do you really think we should tell everyone? What if we panic them?"

"We can't ignore it," Marc insisted, resolving to stand firm. "If there's even a slight chance of danger, we owe it to our families to inform them."

Gaea nodded in agreement, her expression becoming more serious. "Let's gather everyone after dinner. We'll figure out a plan together."

"After we open our presents," Marc added.

Both the Penders and Peppers adopted the European tradition of celebrating Christmas on its eve, sitting around the fireplace. Marc, being from Quebec, had grown up with the tradition.

"After we open the presents, then. We can talk in the arboretum." Gaea suggested.

Marc and Himiko nodded in agreement.

In the kitchen, Vicky greeted Aerin with a warm smile that felt somehow hollow. "I could use an extra pair of hands! We're baking a chocolate cake and gingerbread cookies."

Aerin shrugged, a playful smirk creeping across his lips, though a shadow lingered in his eyes. "I'm always up for an adventure. Let's see how this goes!"

As Aerin plunged into the chaotic whirl of the kitchen, strange shadows danced along the walls, whispering of secrets long buried in the mansion. Just then, Bob and Bill returned from their trip to town, each carrying bags filled with last-minute decorations and gifts. They set to work with an eerie fervor, continuing the transformation of the main living area into a dazzling winter wonderland. Yet, beneath the twinkling lights, an unsettling tension lay thick in the air, like a storm brewing just out of sight.

As evening crept in, the entire Pepper-Pender family gathered in the great room, wrapped in a deceptive sense of unity. Laughter filled the air, but it had an unnatural edge, like ghosts echoing through time. Aerin proudly displayed his first batch of cookies—charmingly misshapen yet absurdly adorned with an excessive amount of bright icing, a bizarre contrast to the dim atmosphere.

"Perfect for Santa!" Vicky giggled, her eyes darting towards a corner of the room as if sensing something lurking just beyond her sight.

As night settled in, the family gathered around the beautifully arranged table, where a feast awaited—a celebration that masked their shared, unspoken fears. They raised their glasses in a heartfelt toast to the season, each sharing their blessings as shadows flickered ominously outside, swirling like wraiths encroaching on their joy and revealing the fragile facade they had built.

After enjoying the meal that Vicky had prepared, the two families returned to the great room and took their seats before the fireplace. Within its massive maw, a fire danced and flickered, casting warm light across the room. Laughter filled the air as presents were unwrapped one by one, unveiling joyful discoveries.

Bob Pepper sat deep in thought, his mind troubled. He often pondered various ideas and situations, and it was he who first brought up the Grimoire and its whereabouts.

"Gaea?" he asked cautiously. "What happened to the book? You didn't sink it in the ocean, did you?"

Gaea glanced nervously at Marc and Himiko. "No, Grandpa," she answered. "We were going to talk to you after we opened presents; talk to all of you. The book is hidden here at the estate. It was nearly taken by two unsavory people. A witch and possibly a warlock, but we were not sure of the other. We think the right thing to do is to seek help at a festival in northern Maine."

"It's an annual gathering of witches and warlocks to celebrate the winter solstice," Himiko added. "There will be people there who know what to do with a book like the Grimoire."

Bill set down the beer he was drinking on the coffee table. He looked like a concerned parent, one who had gone through a lot with his gifted daughter, perhaps too much.

"I thought we were done with this book thing?" he asked. "I don't believe it. How often do we have to go through hell, Gaea?"

His daughter looked down at her cup of cocoa. "I know, Dad, and I'm sorry. I didn't plan any of this."

"Of course not." Cathy had been listening intently and was shocked by the revelation of a situation she thought was resolved. "No one knew the book was in Vicky's restaurant when she bought it."

"We should have emptied the restaurant," Dottie said, standing. "Coffee, anyone?"

"Let me get it, Grandma," Vicky said, also standing.

"You've done enough. Sit." Dottie commanded.

Vicky obeyed reluctantly.

"So, when do you leave for this festival?" Bob asked, picking up a lighter and applying the flame to a cigar. He allowed himself the luxury of tobacco only on very special occasions, such as Christmas Eve.

"Next week," Gaea answered. "Marc, Himiko, and I are driving up for three days. Hopefully, we can find someone we can trust to take the book."

"You're taking the cursed thing?" Bill said, clearly unhappy about their trip.

"No, that would be too dangerous. It will remain hidden."

"What if they come looking for it here?" Cathy asked, clearly concerned.

"It's a possibility, but the chance of that happening is slim to none," Himiko said, taking a sip of her cocoa. "It's well hidden and protected with incantations and common-sense precautions to keep it safe. I don't believe anyone is in danger for now."

"I tend to agree that the book should stay here," Bob said, standing and looking into the fire. "I don't fancy the three of you traveling with it. If you say it's well hidden and safe, I'll go along with it. For Christ's sake, promise me that you three will be careful and keep us updated. If you get into trouble, call. I'll send in the cavalry."

"I still don't like it," Bill complained. "I don't like it one bit, but I suppose there's nothing I can do about it. Where did you hide the book?"

"Better not say," Bob interjected. "It's best if we all remain in the dark concerning that detail."

Cathy nodded her head in agreement. She leaned over and hugged her daughter. "You will be careful?"

Gaea nodded and hugged her mother back. Breaking the embrace, she addressed Marc and Himiko. "We need to plan ASAP."

The trio had a lot to do.

The Grimoire waited deep within the mansion's root cellar, obscured from prying eyes. Its dark bindings absorbed the warmth of its human skin covering, serving as a silent guardian of the secrets it contained. Its pages whispered softly, calling out to unknown persons, awaiting the moment when curiosity would unravel the thin veil between the warmth of family and the chilling reality beneath.

To be continued…

Some Previous Works by Mark E. Welch:

The Widow's Watch: A Haunting on Cape Neddick (1 of 3)

The Widow's Watch: Dreamer's Hideaway (2 of 3)

The Widow's Watch: Shaw Manor (3 of 3)

Tales of the Little Lagoon: Kiwa's Story

The Dream Catcher (A short story)

Spirits and Tales (A short story)

In the works:

Blood of the Winter Solstice:
The Night Witch Series (Book 2)